MY BROTHER'S KEEPER

BOOK II

A Novel

Billie Dureyea Shell

This book is dedicated to:

William Ewell & Sky Holsey, we need more people to do what this sister did. If we want these BullShit police to do there job we going to have to make them, black lives matter but we have to make sure that they also matter to us. If you see a police pull one of your folks over take the time to pull over and get involved the time that you take to let them know that you care about what's going on with your brother's and sisters and that you are your brother's keeper an got there back Just might be what saves their lives. So let's make them respect this black lives matter movement but first it starts by us loving each other and respecting ourselves....... My niggas the revolution will not be televised that doesn't mean we can't keep our own records of what happened let's make this shit count..........

Author
Billie Dureyea Shell

Team Shell

ACKNOWLEDGEMENT

First and foremost I have to give honor to My Lord And Saviour Jesus Christ without him now of this would be possible. 2020 was a MUTHA FUCCA Corona Virus made shit hard 4 niggas but we made it threw y'all keep your head up and know that God got us, no matter they throw in our way no one can stop what God has plan for you...
Its 2021 now FUCC 2020 and Covid 19.... Now to my family momma I love you and you no I got you no matter what. You mean the world 2 me oh and NO MORE PINCHING LOL.

To my little sister Glenda I love you blackie, you No I Got
You always
To my Wife Shatoya Shell you get on my damn nerves
but I wouldnt trade you 4 anything In the world I love
you more then words can ever express. To all my children
I love y'all Jazmine, Ant'Tuan, Davon, Anthony, David,
Lil Dureyea, Alura, Queen Diavion, Cameron,
Preniece, Shaniece and Tajh I love u all and I'll 4ever have ur
back you all give me a reason 2 smile... to my cousin Zane
RIP nigga I miss u more then anyone will ever no, your
always remembered love you bro. to my cousin Ty I miss you
thank 4 looking out 4 me and Zane you played a big part in
my life and I always looked up to you I love you... Uncle
Woody I miss you and love you, you no your my favorite
uncle... To my nigga Jamal love you, my brothers Lawrence
and fred thank 4 showing me the game I love yall 4 that. To
my oldest sister Nedra love you thank you 4 always having my
back. to my family uncles anties cousins etc.. I love y'all even
those of you that act funny as fuck

To my dark side niggas y'all no what it is YAAH GANG....
Now to all my readers and fans I love you thanks for reading I
hope u enjoy this book as much as I enjoy writing
them with this Corona Virus 19 shit there ain't shit to do but
write so l'm on my shit with that being said y'all be safe cover
your face and love each other life is short so love the ones that
really love I'm gone no. enjoy the book

STAY SAFE

Author Billie Dureyea Shell

THERE'S NOTHING U CANNOT DO

IF U PUT UR MIND 2 IT.

All you nigga's got EDD money so aint no excuse

why you can't get a book LOL

PREVIOUSLY IN MY BROTHERS KEEPER -KANE-

"No problem, but I want to see if he's dead. I need to find out something if he's still alive." I got out of the car. It wasn't the same vehicle. Bullet holes covered the surface front to back. The front windshield was shattered and the rear end has a huge dent. Total wreck. I'm grateful to still be on planet earth. Smoke and I approached the gunman. He was barely alive and that's good enough for me. The inside of his mouth filled with blood and his body twitched every five seconds from fighting off death. His clothes were dusty and torn. The collision was devastating. His gun was amazingly still in his grip. I would've been dead if he had enough strength to move. He wasn't in any condition to kill anybody, he failed. Suddenly, he swiftly placed the gun to his head. He would rather kill himself than have one of us take his life. I thought about putting a bullet between his eyes. My trigger finger was itching. Never had I imagined catching a body. Ask me that after seeing Big Bruce for the first time. He's not the type of guy you wanna box on your best day. "Are you The Planner?" I asked sternly. The gunman had a crazy look on his face. He smiled as if he wanted to die. He started coughing up blood while holding the gun pressed to the temple of his head. I glanced at Smoke and he shrugged as if to say, let him. My attention moved back to the gunman. "Where is The Planner?" I became slightly frustrated. He never answered and kept smiling at me like he had no sense. "Do it." Right then, the gun exploded. His brains flew out the side of his head onto the pavement. Shit like this only happened in movies. The driver took his own life. The old Kane would have been shocked. Not after what I've been through. I understand what survival means. If you want the short version... exist.

Shopper's List Kim turned off the car in the mall parking lot. She grabbed her purse from the passenger seat and unplugged her cell phone from the charger. She made a list of things she wanted to purchase. One of the items was a new varsity jacket and hat for Kane. She saw the set two weeks ago when he was on a steady job hunt. The jacket and matching hat had momentarily captured his attention. She noticed how bad he felt after staring at the three hundred dollar price tag. He seemed unhappy. She couldn't imagine how he felt and remembers thinking to herself, when I get the money this will be the first thing I'll buy for my man. He probably feels bad about not having any money. I'll come back in a week when I get paid. Fortunately, things turned out differently. She got out of her Lexus and locked the doors. She planned to leave the clothes in the open so he could see them when he came home. She thought about Kane before herself. She loves him that much. He made her feel better than anyone. If loving him meant robbing a bank or stealing a diamond. It's done. Her love for him will always remain strong. She hurried through the front entrance of the mall. She failed to notice the two men being discreet in the distance. They followed her from the apartment. She didn't prepare for conflict. Her mind was on shopping for her boyfriend. The love of her life. She walked inside the store that had the matching set on display. She was met by the store assistant at the door. The young lady smiled graciously and asked if she needed help finding anything. She looked about sixteen years old with a petite body. She knew why they hired them young and cute with a bright attitude. Eighty percent of the time they could persuade the shopper to buy something. Kim smiled lively at the girl, remembering the time when she was in the same position. "Yes, I do. I'm looking for the varsity jacket and hat that was on display here about two weeks ago." "Oh, I remember." She said kindly. "I think we might have a set in the back. Give me a second to check, please." She hurried off and returned with the varsity gear. It was perfect. "Great," Kim said brightly. I'll take it." She paid and tipped the girl a ten. She spent the next two hours shopping after leaving the store. She made it to the car, carrying four bags, two in each hand. She sat them down and rummaged through her purse for the keys. Suddenly, a powerful force covered her nose and mouth preventing her from breathing. She wasn't able to fight and slowly faded away as the drug took control. The struggle finally ended. Her vision was swallowed by darkness.

Chapter 1
HELP WANTED -KANE-

On the ride back to the apartment. I was trying to conceive what just happened at the warehouse. The Planner sent a trained killer. Smoke and I didn't speak. He probably thought about his share of the money. At this point, we could only imagine that much cash. Everything we had planned was now ruined. I have a diamond worth millions and don't know who else to sell it to. I don't have another buyer. I thought about the bank robbery and the heist. The two crimes I committed after being framed for murder. Trouble seems to follow me around now. I thought for certain things would get better after I sold the rock to The Planner. That's far from happening now. I should have expected a guy like that would try to kill me. The only option I have is to wait for him to call. The thought of putting myself in danger a second time is a shame. I'm asking to die. I adjusted the seat to a more relaxing position and took a deep breath. I don't have a million questions like some people. I only need the answer to one. If somebody can answer me out there in a world people take for granted. I would greatly appreciate it. I didn't expect my life to turn out this way, I was good. I had the best family anyone could ever ask for. Things changed and everything suddenly went south. Why? That's the only question I need someone to answer. Why? The question behind every remark. A simple word that seems to be more of a comeback question. I wonder what my friends would want to know? Smoke would ask about his grandmother. Why did she have to die at sixty-five? Redd, why didn't he have a stronger leg? People recover from leg injuries, but he didn't. Bear would want to know why he had to be the one with a sleeping disorder. He could have been an amazing football player. Kim would ask about not receiving a track scholarship. She was one of the top runners in the state at the time. Many things in life are left unexplained. You just have to take the road that was chosen for you without question. I took the diamond out of my pouch and gave it a mean stare. I turned it side to side. I came close to death two times for this fucking rock. The value of this thing is life-threatening. What the hell was I thinking of when I decided to steal it in the first place? I saw Smoke glance at it. "What do you think we should do?" I broke the silence without looking at him. My attention was on the death rock. "About what?" He asked in a calm voice. "Everything," I whispered. "Starting with this. What do you suggest we do with this damn thing? This... this shit is getting crazy. I mean... what I'm trying to say is... I never pictured us as criminals. Man... we have been best friends since high school. We're supposed to be living it up right now. Running, balling, football, whatever." I felt my emotions taking over. "We were good at everything. The best and nobody could touch us. How can something so good turn out this damn bad?" I felt my blood simmering. Smoke was silent. Maybe he was remembering those moments in high school when we blew out our competition. Somebody is about to get smoked. Two high school state titles in track. That's what the phrase meant. Man... those were the days. Look at the person I've become since then. My father would disown me for what I've done. And he's the one who told me to take care of my mother by any means necessary. The car pulled into the apartments. I was ready to get out when Smoke spoke up. "Kane, we do what we have to do. You're smarter than you think. I trusted you with the bank and the museum heist. Call me insane, but I didn't do it because you're my friend. I did it because I believe in you." He smiled. I closed my fist and gave my best friend some dap. I needed that. I went into the apartment feeling better. Kim wasn't home. I was exhausted from everything that happened today. I walked directly to the bedroom and crashed on the bed. Now I know how tired you can get from a gun battle.

Chapter 2
WAKE UP CALL

"How do I catch the ball?" I asked. "It's bigger than me." My father walked over and showed me how to spread my fingers. He was teaching me how to catch a football. "Keep your finger's apart son and when the ball comes in your direction. Wrap your hands around it, ok?" I held my hands out with my fingers spread just like he told me. "But... I'm scared." He walked about ten yards away from me. I followed close behind and made it two yards before he told me to stop. He said I'm supposed to be a few feet away. I had to stay put and catch an enormous ball. "There's no reason to be scared, son. The ball won't hurt you." I held my hands out while still trying to follow my father. The helmet felt too big for my head. My skull felt heavier than before. I couldn't see straight with it covering my eyes. I wanted to take it off. I felt a sudden sting in my stomach. "Ouch!" He had thrown the ball and it hit me in the center of my chest. I wasn't ready for it and I started to cry. I left the ball on the ground and walked in his direction. When I made it to him, the air in my three-year-old chest slowly returned. He ran in the opposite direction towards the ball. The oversized helmet caused me to walk off-balance. My hands were in a catch position as I followed behind him. The blow to my chest brought tears to my eyes. I didn't like the football game we were playing. I wanted to stop. I felt the ball hit my hands. It stung a little, but not like the first time. I continued forward with my hands out and tripped face forward over the ball. "Ouch." My hands hit the ground. The helmet felt like a block of stone and I collapsed on the ground. Grass and dirt got in my mouth. It was hard to get up. I thought my father was walking over to pick me up. Instead, he grabbed the football and ran in the opposite direction. Somewhere, the distinct sound of my brother laughing could be heard. His voice was clear and not inspiring. I got up from the ground and noticed my father standing in the distance. For some reason, my hands were out with my fingers spread apart. I walked towards him. "I hate foo..." I felt a sting in my hands. The world around me became silent. The sound of my brother laughing, couldn't be heard anymore. I was no longer crying as I continued walking towards my father, ready to end my football career in three catch attempts. I opened my eyes to see if he was in front of me. Surprisingly, I saw my hands wrapped around the football. I caught it! I approached my father and spiked the ball on the ground. He picked me up and tossed me into the air while cheering. He sounded proud of me. "You caught the ball son! That's my boy." Maybe that was all the inspiration I needed. I caught the football for the first time in my life at the age of three. What a birthday. A loud sound woke me from my dream. I remembered that day vividly. I didn't drop a football again until my sophomore year of high school. Only because I collided with another receiver on the team while going after the ball simultaneously. His fault if you want to know the truth. My side of the field, my route. That was my final season before I got arrested for murder. I looked at the clock, 3:45 am. The alarm sounded. I set the timer when I was searching for a job and forgot to turn it off. I rolled over to get some more rest. Something didn't feel quite right. I checked the time again to assure there was no confusion, 3:46 am. I set up. Strange, I didn't notice this before, Kim was not in the bed.

Chapter 3
MISSING PERSON

My curiosity level rose every second. "Where's Kim?" I felt like a bag of bones. My body, put up a fight as I got out of bed. I had to command my legs to operate. They felt paralyzed. I walked off the numb feeling heading into the living room. I needed some water immediately. My mouth was dry as the Arizona desert. My mind went back to Kim. Perhaps she went out with a friend? That suggestion spent a short amount of time in my mind. No way, she's not the stay out type. Work? Another suggestion that wasn't the right answer. Damn, where could she have gone? I was beginning to seriously worry about her whereabouts. I finished the glass of water. It helped a little. At least my cottonmouth was gone. This had to be how my father felt about my mother. Welcome to stress. There's a possibility she stayed out cheating with another guy. I smiled at that. Perfect time to do it when I gained forty grand in cash and a diamond worth millions. Ok, I shouldn't think about her that way. That was stupid. Damn, I'm getting desperate. I left the kitchen and sat in complete darkness in the living room. If I didn't know any better, I resembled an angry husband, waiting in the middle of the night for his cheating wife to come home. Is this how married people act? Apparently so. My eyes were wide, anticipating her to walk through the door at any moment. What other alternative do I have? Maybe, I should have stayed home. The Planner tried to kill me and now Kim is suddenly missing. I don't know what to think or how to feel. "Shit," I whispered. I thought back to when I switched my phone on vibrate after Smoke and I left the restaurant. How did I forget something like that? What if she tried to call my phone? I hurried to the bedroom. I picked up my pants and grabbed my phone from the left pocket. No, it was dead. I drained the battery. Charger. Where is it? I never misplace it. Now it's gone. Shit. Where did I put that damn thing? I search the entire bedroom with sonic boom speed. I couldn't find it anywhere. Ok, calm down. The living room? I frantically checked the entire area. I felt my heart rate speed up to 200 mph. My adrenaline took over. This could be important. What if something serious happened? I stopped searching to gather my thoughts. I could have a heart attack at the speed I was moving. Think, where was the last place you charged your phone? I didn't, Kim used it. She needs a new one so she borrowed mine. Bedroom, living room, kitchen? She used it in the kitchen. I hurried to the kitchen. Bingo. Right there in front of my face. My charger was plugged into the wall. I connected it to my phone and waited a minute before it gained some power. I had seven missed calls. None were from Kim. What, why? I called her phone five times. Each call ended in her voicemail. I sat on the sofa perplexed. I accidentally turned on the TV by sitting on the remote control. The news turned on. "Oh, my God." Kim's car had been abandoned at the mall. The news headline read, Possible Missing Person.

Chapter 4
THE BLUES

That was something I thought would never happen in my life. Someone kidnapped Kim. Four shopping bags were left behind as evidence. The keys to her car were found in the keyhole of the driver's side door. This is all my fault. What did she do to deserve this? She is my world and I put her in danger. My mind raced at an unbelievable speed. My hands started shaking uncontrollably. My head felt like Mike Tyson gave me a touch up. I thought about what I need to do to bring her home. The police won't be able to help if I go to them. Damn, things keep getting worse. I wish I could take it all back. If my father was alive, my path would have been different. What would he have done in this situation? My heart started to ache. This is worse than a demon snatching my soul. I kept in mind not to fold under pressure. I need to be strong for Kim. She needs me. I have to figure this shit out immediately because her life could be in even more danger. I sat on the couch and my body sank into the pillows. I backtracked, thinking of a few possibilities that led up to the kidnapping. Ok, did I provoke someone from the bank robbery to go after Kim? That question had an easy answer. The diamond brought up a five million dollar reason, The Planner. He tried to kill me for the rock. Arranging a kidnapping is something I should have expected when dealing with an animal. I balled my fists, infuriated just thinking about it. I felt my nails digging into my palms. The fucking Planner. How did he know about Kim? If he found me, he could find her. He is the one. The diamond for my girlfriend, that's a fair trade. I sat on the thought longer than an Indy 500 race. It was difficult finding a reason why The Planner could be the wrong person to suspect. What if the kidnapping was random? Hard to make a case for that in my situation. The bottom line is he took her to get back at me. The guy in the BMW worked for him. He planned this beforehand in case his henchman failed. I was dumb and gullible. Man, I began to feel dizzy just thinking about it. I let my guard down and left Kim vulnerable. That monster had watched my every move. I assume he followed us back to the apartment from the museum. I came to the realization that this is not a dream. The only way to wake up from this reality of a nightmare is to save Kim. I have the diamond in my possession. He won't harm her while I have it.

At least, that is what I'm praying for. This doesn't have to involve violence if he wants to trade. The money is no longer a concern. Kim is the only thing that matters. I don't care if she never forgives me. I want her returned home safely. I leaned back on the couch and sighed. This is now personal. The only thing I can do is wait for The Planner to call with a trade offer. After I get her back... he's dead and I put that on my father's grave.

Chapter 5

NO PLACE LIKE HOME

Kim was blindfolded and tied to a bed. She woke up and couldn't see anything and became frightened, sweat dripped down her forehead into the blindfold. Her eyes were covered in darkness. Nothing could be heard, the room fell completely silent. The sound of her breath enhanced in her ears. She struggled to move her hands and feet. The bonds were tight, she was trapped. She whimpered for help, the gag in her mouth prevented her from yelling. She burned her wrists after trying to free herself. The rope had rubbed against her skin. The sensation in both wrists became unbearable and it forced her to give up. It was hard to remember how she got in this predicament. Her mind only thought of freedom. She blocked out how excruciating the pain felt in her wrists. If she wanted to survive, she had to use her brain. She thought about the situation, kicking and screaming wouldn't help. The darkness provided a calm silence of emotional thinking. Her breathing suddenly increased. She had an emotional breakdown after not being able to perceive the truth. Tears streamed past the dimples in her cheeks. She didn't understand why something, unexpectedly like this would happen to her. The thought of being held captive by an unknown person created even more fear in her heart. Ninety percent of women who were kidnapped didn't survive. She began to panic and became wildly out of control. Freedom surfaced over death. The amount of strength in her body proved useless against the bonds. The burning sensation returned and it forced her to stop a second time. Her wrists and ankles were on fire. The rope ate through her skin and caused each point of contact to bleed. She submitted after coming up with nothing helpful. A memory flashed in her mind of when she had left the apartment. She recalled walking into the mall to purchase some clothes for Kane, then walking back to her car. She started crying, what happened next resurfaced vividly. The moment was hard to grasp. It changed her life. I was kidnapped in the mall parking lot. Somebody grabbed her from behind, then darkness. The person could be a serial killer, who target beautiful women. Why, she thought. The bank robbery? The diamond? Her mind traveled back to high school when she could run around the track, free and happy. Suddenly, she heard footsteps on a wooden floor. The sound of the doorknob turning entered her ears. Two male voices could be heard in the room. A great amount of anxiety took over her body. She heard one say. "Let me have her Black Bandit?" "No Ali, leave us." "But-" "No buts," A stern voice interrupted. The door closed. She listened to footsteps as they approach the bed. She could only hear the person breathing as his presence hovered over her body. She heard a belt unbuckle and drop to the floor. She frantically struggled with the bond as did the feeling of being unsafe intensified. The person suddenly grabbed her by the legs and pulled down her underwear. No, she thought. Please God, no. His body weighed down on her. He wrapped one hand around her neck and forced himself inside.

Chapter 6
THE GAME

After thirty minutes of torture, he finished. It felt like a century. Kim was unable to stop the predator. Her mind shattered into tiny pieces of sadness. She searched for a reason to live. Someone took advantage of her and it felt like the most horrible way to feel in the world. Her wrists and ankles were scarred after they were burned by the rope. She could feel a bruise from the tight chokehold he had on her neck. The process of being helpless at the time caused her to cry. She heard the man pants pull up and belt buckle. She listened quietly to everything happening in the room. The sound of his footsteps walking away told her the assault was over. The door opened and closed. Nobody inside, but her. Troubled thoughts competed with her heartbeat. Breathing became hard. Making it out alive crossed her mind. She wanted to live and not give up. Tough out one of the worst predicaments. Whatever it would take to prevail. She decided to fight for her life. She wanted to see her friends again. Kane, welcoming her with a warm hug every time she came home. The thought of not having him felt like a sword that slowly pierced her heart. She was interrupted by movement outside of the room. The door opened, footsteps entered. Her heart started pounding. Please, not again! She heard the voice of a woman. "Get her off the bed and bring her down to the van. Bandit wants to move her." "I want to have fun with her first." A man spoke. "No," The woman demanded. "The van is waiting, we need to get her off the premise. I don't care what happens to her after that." "It won't take that long." He rebelled. She heard a very loud slap. "What did I tell you, Ali? You're a damn fool. Get this bitch to the van." "Ok." He cried. Kim felt a hand untie the first restrain. She had begun to move, but there was no reason to panic. Her legs and arms were about to be free. Find a weapon, she thought. He would underestimate her speed and agility. She listened to him bicker under his breath. She felt his hand massage her clitoris. The thought of his disgusting touch made her body twitch. He had held down her free hand, she wanted to slap him harder than the other woman had done. To her surprise, she came back into the room, answering her prayer. "Ali," She yelled. "What's taking you so long? Don't get Bandit agitated by being stupid. Hurry." "These damn knots are tight and giving me a hard time." He lied.

"Please, my grandmother can untie those knots. That girl is worth more than a cheap fuck, thirty-five million dollars. Act like you want a piece of the money. Now bring your ass before Bandit decides to deal with you." "Ok, ok." Kim heard the woman leave the room. The predator had swiftly removed his hand when she entered. She sighed, feeling relieved by not reliving a second assault. The man started to untie the next knot from around her other wrist. I need a weapon, She thought about the van which would be her next destination. She had to be careful not to make any mistakes. Her second hand dropped freely, then a leg. One more knot, she thought. She hesitated for a short moment, scared of what might happen. She activated, now free to take action. She had to be swift. The blindfold removed from her eyes, the gag in her other hand, blurry vision. The man grabbed her, too late. She saw the surroundings of the room. Her eyes captured terrifying images of a familiar place.

Chapter 7
POKE, POKE

Kim had to force her body to work. The room shocked her, but she had to act immediately or die. Different kinds of emotions spun around in her head. This isn't real, she thought. A picture sitting on the nightstand with two familiar faces smiled back at her. Why did it have to be in this house? She would visit often in the summer. The bed that momentary restrained her body from moving belonged to the Simmons. The man in front of her made a move. The fight was on, no more crying. Anger ruled over every other emotion. Her life was on the line. She threw multiple punches and fought off the guy the woman called, Ali. A rather skinny and weak kid. After he fell to the floor, she sprung from the bed. To see a familiar face wrecked her nerves. She had to remain focused. Time was running out. She kicked the guy on the floor and he folded like a baby. She reached over to the nightstand and grabbed a pencil. It was sharp and the perfect size to conceal in her designer belt. She had found a weapon, but knew making it out of the house without getting caught would be difficult. The door opened, interrupting her short moment of freedom. She was shocked by the man standing in front of her. Abel... He caused the pain she felt. It left a blank look on her face. She was unable to feel anything emotionally after discovering the brother of her lover. The thought of informing Kane of his brother made her teary-eyed. Abel, you fucking monster. She lost herself in thought and couldn't react in time to a swift backhand. She fell back on the bed and waited patiently to be tied up again. She formed a plan of attack for when they were settled in the van. Abel looked at Ali down on the floor in a fetal position. "Get up," He grabbed him by the shirt with one hand and lifted him off the floor. "Go start the van. Can I trust you to do that?" Ali felt Abel's amazing strength for the first time. He had manhandled him off the floor like a small puppy. "Sorry." His toes were barely touching the surface. "I can start the van." He held out a hand, scared for his life. Abel terrified him. After a long pause, his feet flattened on the wooden floor. His knees slightly buckled under his weight while catching his balance. The key to the van dropped in the palm of his hand. "The damage is done," Abel muttered. "I'll put her in the van." "Abel," Kim sat up on the bed. Tears slowly rolled down her cheeks.

"Kane will find out what you did to me." Abel smirked. "I think he'll be even more satisfied to find out what I did to his father." He backhanded her with enough power to force her head to the side. It was loud enough to be heard downstairs. "Unfortunately, you'll be dead." He retied her hands and feet. Kane will find out soon, he thought. The information dropped on Kim was heavy, Abel murdered their father. He hoisted her from the bed. The side of her face pounded in pain. She stood there and waited for an order. Her emotions were high. He had committed two hideous acts. Rape and murder, she felt dirty and cheated. The feeling intensified after thinking of their father. He put the gag back in her mouth and pushed her forward. She walked out of the door. Kane's room was down the hall. She would have to pass by to reach the stairs. Abel guided her down the hall. She closed her eyes to avoid looking at the pictures along the way. She felt the presence of Kane's room. The door was open and she forced herself not to look inside. She walked through the rest of the house staying focused on the van. The plan didn't change, the fight wasn't over. Abel said, she would be dead. That statement didn't work for her, she would make it back to Kane, alive. Abel stopped Kim on the side of the van and opened the door. "Get in." She did and he shut it behind her. He got in the front passenger seat. He gave Ali a certain look to let him know, he fucked up. He planned to find a place to kill Kim and dump the body. The van began to move. Both men were quiet. Kim sat patiently, waiting for the perfect time to strike. She felt good, Abel didn't search her belt. The second part of her plan, fight for your life. Ali drove, she decided to take him out first. She had to be a fighter. Not only for herself, but for all women. She slowly maneuvered her hands from behind her back to the side of her belt. They were heading down a two-lane road. She successfully slipped the pencil out unnoticed. Traffic moved freely on the opposite side of the street. Perfect time to attack. She moved with extraordinary speed and stabbed the sharp piece of wood halfway in Ali's neck.

Chapter 8
CRASH, BANG

Ali tried to yell out, but the pencil jabbed halfway through his neck prevented him from doing so. Kim swiftly removed the gag while setting her sights on Abel. She maneuvered to the opposite side where she had the advantage. The van swerved back and forth through traffic. Ali released the steering wheel and grabbed his neck. Abel tried to gain control of the vehicle by holding onto the wheel with his left hand. He had a gun stashed in the glove box. He reached for the compartment with his free hand. Kim had her arm wrapped around his neck, making it difficult. She positioned her knees against the seat and pulled back. The method applied an extreme amount of pressure on Abel's neck. Her hands were still tied together, making the chokehold even more impressive. She sensed his energy slowly declining, he wasn't as strong as before. Abel could barely breathe. He decided not to focus on Kim.

Avoiding a head-on collision became more important. He thought about it again as he felt the need to pass out. Blowing her head off wouldn't satisfy him anymore. He decided to slowly torture her if he got through this situation. He saw Ali's eyes roll to the back of his head like he was the Undertaker. Blood gushed out of his neck and oozed down his fingers. Ali had suffered a deadly blow through his esophagus. Damn, he thought. He concentrated on keeping the wheel steady. Kim applied a respectful amount of pressure. He had to rely on his mental strength. The seat had been adjusted back before he got inside the van to compensate for his height. He reached to the side and pulled the lever. The seat slid forward enough to pop the glove box. The compartment door fell freely. What the fuck, he thought. The clip wasn't in the gun. He leaned back to release some of the pressure on his neck. Trying to put the weapon together with one hand would be difficult. He focused on the road. The van slightly swerved on and off the street. He glanced at Ali, the computer genius was dead. Road, glove compartment, road. He could only commit to one. He could put the clip in the gun if he removed his hand off the wheel. Not killing himself while trying would be a problem. He heard multiple horn sounds from other vehicles as they past. He needed to do something and dying wasn't an option. The van shook violently off-road. Abel's balance had him all over the place. A bullet would definitely go in her head. He reached for the gun and placed it between his legs. His air supply was completely gone. Next, he had to grab the clip. Come on, almost... got it. He felt seconds away from choking to death. He had never held air in his lungs longer than two minutes. The timer had approached two and a half minutes. He successfully put the clip in the gun after the road smoothed out. Finally. He held the weapon, but it still wasn't ready. It had to be loaded, which would require a greater effort. He leaned back and felt her stranglehold ease on his neck. His first thought, focus on the road. His fingertips barely controlled the steering wheel. A fast incoming vehicle came into view. He swerved the van into the proper lane. The maneuver caused Ali to fall over his lap. His weight covered Abel's hand that held the pistol. Fuck. He swiftly reached his left arm out to regain control of the van. Ali had briefly knocked his hand off the steering wheel. His body was in an awkward position. He felt overwhelmed by trying to keep everything in control at the same time. The vehicle swerved into the wrong lane. A car headed straight for them. The driver dodged the van, saving his own life. Abel heard the sound of a horn blow several times. The road was clear. He had a split second to load the gun. One hand wouldn't get the job done, he made up his mind. He swiftly released the wheel and lifted Ali's body from over his hand. He had a firm grip on the pistol. Loading the chamber sounded good to his ears. Suddenly, the van swerved out of control into oncoming traffic. He didn't have time to reposition the vehicle, it collided with another car and flipped upside-down. Pain covered his entire body. Death knocked at the front door. He blocked it out of his mind, knowing he had to vacate the scene. He slowly crawled from under the van military-style, feeling like he already died. Kim would have to meet death at a later time. The gun still in his hand as he escaped. He could barely come to a full stand. His groan turned into a roar that could be heard through the trees. He made it out alive. A vehicle slid to a stop in front of the accident. Abel approached the stopped car. The man in the vehicle offered help. Abel aimed his pistol through the window and took the innocent man hostage.

Chapter 9
GRADY -KANE-

I've been up all night waiting for The Planner to call. I glanced at the clock on the wall. It was nine in the morning and felt as if time decided to drag. I called my boys an hour ago. Smoke, Redd, and Bear were on the way over to help find a solution. It's killing me on the inside not knowing if something bad was happening to Kim. I need to know if she's safe. The Planner is dead if he's the person behind this. I don't need a second opinion. I got into some serious shit when I decided to steal the diamond. The money blinded me. I put my family in danger, thinking foolishly. I'm ok if something happened to me, not Kim. I wouldn't be able to forgive myself. I would have to embrace that failure forever. I have to kill this psychopath. I looked at my phone. It was fully charged. The battery life bars were green. I had turned the ringer on the highest volume. No calls. Where the hell is he? Kim for the diamond. That's easy enough to handle, no need to wait. So what's the holdup? My doorbell rung. I got up and looked through the peephole. My boys were standing behind the door. I greeted each of them individually as they walked past the threshold. "Sup Smoke." I gave my best friend some dap. "Sup," Smoke held a sincere look on his face. "Man, I'm sorry about what happened. I saw the news this morning." "Thanks," I said. "What's good Redd, Bear?" I gave them some dap. "Nothin' much," Redd spoke up first. "Just trying to show some support. We'll figure this mess out. Believe that." "Thanks," I told him. "We got your back my dawg," Bear said. "Thanks, big man." I told him. I spoke to all of them. "I appreciate you guys for coming. I really need your support to get through this. I'm down and don't know what to do with myself." I tried not to get emotional. It was hard not to have a mental breakdown. They know me and that wasn't apart of acting soft. Kim and I have been together for a very long time. She is the love of my life, the beautiful woman in my love story. And my boys are like family to her. We all have a connection. I would do the same for one of them. Be there when they need me most. Everyone seated in the living room. I went into the kitchen to get a bottle of Vodka. I needed a sip of something other than water. Smoke spoke up first. "Do you think this has something to do with that shootout?" "Shootout?" Redd asked. "Y'all were in a shootout?" "Yep," I began to elaborate on the story. "We were supposed to meet with The Planner to get the money for the diamond, simple exchange. I got in the car with a guy he sent to meet me before our deal. Smoke tailed the vehicle to watch my back. The guy spotted him and thought it was a setup. I think he planned to kill me after I gave him the diamond. We went to war with a straight-up lunatic. I had to bang him with the rear end of the car to stop him. He was pretty fucked up afterward. Still alive, though. I asked about The Planner and he shot himself in the head, just like that." "Damn," Bear awed. "Word," Redd added. "No, bullshit." I assured them. "Cold-blooded." My phone rung. I downed a shot of Vodka before rushing into the living room. "Yo." "You blew it." A harsh radio voice came through the receiver. I knew exactly who was on the other end. The Planner. "No mu'fucka, you blew it. You tried to have me dropped off... And you kidnapped my girl." I was furious and shouldn't have spoken to him that way, Kim's safety is more important. I had every eye in the room, pinned on me. I held their full attention. After a long moment of silence, he spoke. "Are you ready to stop pouting?" I didn't respond and he continued. "First and foremost, I told you to come by yourself and you failed to do so. Did you plan to have my driver setup? Not to mention, he died for my cause. Second, I didn't kidnap your little bitch." What, that took me by surprise. "Then who did?" I asked. "I don't have a clue," he said. "Although, I'll help you find her for one million." "Out of the money for the diamond?" Kim is worth more than money to me. I would've given him the diamond for the information. "Why not," he said. "I don't see this ending any other way after what happened with my driver. A small price for my loss. I'll give you a call when I have the information you need." He hung up the phone. What just happened? He didn't have Kim? I talked with my boys while we waited in the living room until six in the afternoon when he finally called my phone. "Turn on the six o'clock news," he said before ending the call. I did and my eyes saw a freak accident on the screen. I read the news headline. MISSING WOMAN FOUND IN LIFE-THREATENING ACCIDENT. VICTIM IS GETTING TREATMENT AT GRADY HOSPITAL.

Chapter 10
CHECK-IN TIME

After I read the headline on the six o'clock news, I blacked out. I grabbed the nearest keys I could find and bolted from the apartment. I heard Smoke yell out I grabbed the wrong keys. It didn't matter to me. I was on my way to Grady no matter whose car I drove. Kim is in the hospital. I didn't bother waiting around to hear what story they assume happened. My main priority is making it to her. I turned the car alarm off and opened the door. Surprisingly, Smoke got in the passenger seat. I thought he was about to seriously lose his mind. His eyes were wide when he asked what I'm waiting for? I told you he's fast. He wanted to know if Kim was ok. She's like his little sister. The Audi fired up and I swiftly put the vehicle in reverse. Redd and Bear were way too slow to match our speed. Waiting for them didn't cross my mind as I peeled out. The tires performed a burnout when my foot floored the pedal. I was on a mission. My mind raced faster than the car. I'm glad Smoke came along with me. If something serious happened to Kim. I'll need some kind of support. I'll call Redd and Bear when we reach the hospital. Anxiety took over my body for the entire ride. I pleaded with God for Kim to be alright and for the authorities not to pull us over. We made it to Grady in twenty minutes. I skidded the car to a stop at the emergency entrance. I got out with the vehicle still running. Thankfully, Smoke took care of it. I ran through the automatic doors to the front desk. The lady sitting there thought I was crazy. I could tell by the look on her face. "Can you tell me what room Kimberly Jones is in?" The woman held up a sign-in sheet. "Here, fill this out and wait to be called." Without thinking and already feeling like a madman, I slapped the damn clipboard from her hand. "I don't have any fucking time to waste on a piece of paper, lady." "Oh my God." She said hysterically. "Security!" Smoke entered the hospital at this time. What I did was wrong. I let my emotions get the best of me. I noticed a security guard approaching us from down the hall. I turned to the woman with a sincere look on my face. "Listen... I'm sorry. I didn't mean for that to happen. Please forgive me? I'm here for my wife. She was brought here after getting into a bad accident. I'm very emotional. Please understand what I'm going through." "Is there a problem?" The security guard asked. The woman looked at me and I whispered. "Please, I love her." Just quiet enough for her to hear. The anger on her face turned into an emotional heartfelt sadness. She felt what I said. Her next words brought an extraordinary amount of life back to my soul. "There's no problem." She answered the guard. "She's in room 205." "Thank you so much." I picked up the sign-in sheet and completed it. Smoke did the same before handing it back to her. "Sorry again." "Don't worry about it, honey. I know you're in love." She turned to the security guard. "Edward, can you show them to room 205?" "Yes, ma'am." He said. We followed the security guard to the elevator. We took it to the second floor and got off. The security guard stayed on and pointed in the direction towards the room. We were in the 200 hallway. Five rooms down and Kim would be behind that door. It felt like the hallway got longer after every step I took. I thought about a million and one things that could have gone wrong as we approached the room. I hesitated after grabbing the doorknob. My life flashed before my eyes. I glanced at Smoke and saw a concerned look on his face. He probably thought if I went crazy to check me into a room. Three things you immediately understand when in a hospital. Either you work there, came to visit, or you're there for treatment. I took a deep breath to prepare myself before I walked into the room. After I took the first step in, I knew it was Kim. She appeared to be lifeless.

Chapter 11
PRESSURE

I felt faint and stopped in the middle of the room. My legs wouldn't move forward and I lost control of my body. I failed to notice the doctor and another man wearing a long overcoat standing next to Kim's bed. Smoke bumped into me from behind. You would've thought I was a statue. I felt paralyzed. I had a feeling every eye in the room was on me. My eyes focused on Kim lying in bed, hooked up to all kinds of wires. I blinked a couple of times to make sure I'm not trapped in a bad dream. The doctor in the room approached me. He spoke, but I couldn't hear a word he said. I looked straight through him with as if he weren't there. My soul had left my body empty. Smoke shook my shoulder a few times trying to bring me back to reality. I finally heard what the doctor say. "Excuse me, sir. Are you related to this young lady?" "Yes, sir. I'm her husband and this is her cousin. We checked in with the lady at the front desk. She should be calling soon." I told him. The lady at the front desk spoke through the intercom and the doctor cleared us. "Thank you." He said to the lady over the speaker. He turned to us. "You guys are fine. If you have any questions, feel free to ask." I walked over to the bed and stood next to it. I couldn't take my eyes off Kim. She had no movement in her body. She appeared to be in a deep sleep. I studied her face long and hard. I didn't notice before, but it was bruised. What happened? A monster did this to the one I love. My mind went blank. I noticed the man in the overcoat staring at me as if he knew my life story. I whispered to the doctor, barely getting the words out because my emotions were in control. "What happened... to her?" I wasn't prepared for what he was about to say. "She was in a horrific accident." He approached me and placed his hand on my shoulder. "There's more," He took his hand off my shoulder and turned to Kim. He had a sense of concern in his voice. "She was raped." My state of mind changed after his last statement. I felt an unanticipated amount of adrenaline and rage. I could've destroyed everything in the room. Those words hit me like a shotgun to the head. I didn't expect the old Kane to continue living in my body. I changed into another person. A murderous persona invaded my mind. I became determined to find out who did this to my queen. I walked around to the side of the bed and leaned in closer to Kim.

I gracefully brushed her hair to the side with my hand. "How long has she been asleep?" "Since she arrived." He told me. "What, since... she's got here?" Something told me this wasn't good. "Sir, the accident put her in a coma. We're not sure if she'll be able to recover." The doctor held his head down. Coma, not able to recover. Shit just kept getting worse. Life without Kim is something I couldn't imagine. First, my father and now the love of my life. I couldn't respond to the doctor. My heart shattered. His words crushed me. She was kidnapped, raped, and in a coma with a possibility of not waking up. I felt my eyes beginning to water. "Who?" I whispered. That's all I had the strength to say. The doctor didn't have an answer and left the room. Smoke was sitting down with his head down in his hands, slowly shaking his head from side to side. The man in the overcoat spoke up. "Kane Simmons, correct?" "Who are you?" I asked. "And how do you know my name?" "I know exactly who you are Mr. Simmons. Do you remember when we met two years ago?" He reached inside his coat. I stared at the man for a moment. He looked like an ordinary white guy with blond hair and blue eyes. I couldn't place him. "No, I'm sorry I can't recall when we met." He flipped open his wallet. I immediately noticed a shiny badge. "Agent Chase with the FBI. You can call me, Rick. Two years ago, my partner and I came to your school and arrested you. Well, we tried, but you ran. Later, you were on trial for the murder of a teacher and was proven not guilty. I'm also currently investigating the murder of your father." "I remember," I whispered thinking back to the day. "So, what are you doing here if you're working my father's case?" "You tell me? You were on trial for murder. Your father was killed and your girlfriend was kidnapped. You don't think everything that has happened is connected? I'm also aware of your mother's condition. Not to mention, a man was murdered yesterday. And here's the good part. A witness saw you get into a black BMW with the guy after leaving a restaurant on 17th street."

Chapter 12
THE OFFICE

The news from agent Rick shocked me. I wasn't prepared and I looked at Smoke for an answer. He had frog eyes and I could tell the news took him by surprise. I was hesitant to speak. I wanted to choose my next words carefully. There's no doubt in my mind this officer is about to take me back to jail. Rick spoke up before I could give him an answer. "Listen, kid. I know what you're going through. I understand. I'm not here to arrest you. That guy who was killed yesterday was a professional hitman named Ke'Mo Cut. The FBI had been searching for him for ten years. He was the top criminal on our list. You're very lucky to still be breathing. He was wanted dead or alive with a $500,000 reward stamped on his head. Now, if you were the one to put him down or not, it doesn't benefit me any. The FBI is covering up his death anyway they can, to avoid paying the bounty which benefits them. The BMW on the crime scene was destroyed of all evidence. They washed the whole thing away like it never happened. We have the power to handle matters like that. It happens all the time, so you have nothing to worry about. Moving along, I'm here to question you about your father and Mrs. Jones." I sighed. Damn, I thought a prison cell had my name on it. They were getting my bunk made up for me. I was relieved that going back to jail wasn't my fate for today. Another day of freedom, what a coincidence. The officer who arrested me is investigating my father's murder and working on Kim's case. It's like he's a part of my life. "So what do you need to know?" "Let's start with your father." He said. "Do you know anything about the business he was conducting outside of work? For instance, he would fly out of the country every two months." "No, I don't. I was unaware he worked outside of his office. Does that have something to do with his death?" I had a question of my own. "That's what I'm here to find out." He said while looking down at a notepad and taking notes. "The money your father made out of the county is unaccounted for. I did some investigation on his travels. Your father flew under a different alias, Bill Right. He made large money transactions under that name. There are more unidentified purchases, but I never discovered what they were. They were unable to be traced. You know of anyone who threatened or wanted to harm your father?" I couldn't comprehend what my father was doing. Bill Right? I wonder if my mother knew anything about his travels or different alias. "Come again?" "Do you know of anyone who wanted to harm your father?" His pen was ready to jot down my next words. "No, there's no one I can think of at the moment. Everyone loved my father. He had no enemies." I assured him. He acknowledged me by nodding his head. "Ok, that's all I needed to ask about your father. I have a couple of questions about your girlfriend. I'll get straight to the point. Do you know a man named Alfred Ben?" I shook my head from side to side. "No, why you ask?" "Well, when we arrived at the scene of the accident." He elaborated. "Kim was bonded at the hands with rope. Mr. Ben was the driver of the vehicle and was found dead with a pencil stabbed halfway through his neck. He took part in the kidnapping. It was a specific kind of pencil with gold letters that read, Yale University. They give one to each of their new enrollments. I checked the school enrollment list and Mr. Ben is currently an active student. I also recognized that he was involved in a rape and murder case of his own with a young lady who was a student at the university. His father, who is an alumnus, had money to make it disappear. He blew out the case and his son was found not guilty. What I'm trying to get at is the semen found in Mrs. Jones and the DNA from Mr. Ben didn't match. He didn't commit the rape. There's someone else involved." "I don't have a clue who did this to her. If I knew of anyone who wanted to kidnap and ra... " I couldn't get the words out. My emotions took over. "I would... " He cut me off. "I already know. Here, take my card. If anything comes to mind or you have any questions, don't hesitate to call." He left the room. I placed the card in my pocket. I looked at Kim one more time and kissed her forehead. I had some investigating to do of my own. I have to go back to my father's office.

Chapter 13
NICE WORK

Abel felt an extreme amount of pain throughout his body. Apparently, Ali wasn't efficient enough with handling Kim. He got himself killed. Following the accident, Abel embraced the thought of how he would take care of her while she's in the hospital. His plan was ruined. Trading her for the diamond was out of the question. Ali knocked that ball right out of the park. He turned on the TV to watch the news. The report about the accident was on. His body ached every time he moved. He leaned back in what used to be his father's favorite resting chair. He knew Kim was in critical condition. It would benefit him if she died. He wanted to kill her after exiting the vehicle. Unfortunately, that wish was unanswered. Too many witnesses and not enough time. He didn't have enough strength and had to vacate the scene. Arranging her murder sat on his mind. A security blanket if he doesn't want to get caught. There's a slight possibility she could wake up from the coma. She would provide enough evidence against him to send the cops. She had seen everything. The mansion, my mother's room, Ali, and most of all... me, he thought. She would tell the cops he kidnapped and the raped her, which will convict him after a DNA test. Doctors had a way of finding out when a woman was raped. They had obtained his semen. He went through different scenarios in his mind. Damn, he thought. Not good. She'll run her mouth. Something has to be done. They would eventually find him and test his DNA. The rest would be history. If he doesn't get to Kim before she's out of the coma. He can kiss his life goodbye. A life behind bars was not part of his world dominance plan. For the rest of his life, he would be on the run. And that's exactly what he'll do, run. He reached over to the table and grabbed a pack of cigarettes. His tenth since arriving two hours ago. He had to take care of the hostage, then burn the vehicle before returning home. A bullet to the head, quick execution. Abel lit his cigarette and leaned back in the chair. Time to think. What to do, what to do? He blew out a ring of smoke. His great mind went to work. Gina emerged into the room looking like a lovely kind of death that only he could appreciate. She walked over to him. "Is there anything I can do for you my, love?" He blew out another ring of smoke. He thought about how she could help. So beautiful and smart, he thought. You wouldn't be able to fathom the amount of destruction and death she could cause. "Yes, you can. The woman from this morning is being held at Grady Hospital. The accident left her in a coma. I need to figure out a way to infiltrate the facility and kill her. Have any suggestions?" She smiled seductively and stood over him. She loved scheming and bringing death to others. It was becoming a common thing with her. Killing a person aroused her sexually. She sat on Abel's lap, facing him. She took the cigarette from his mouth and took a puff. "I'll take care of her for you." She blew smoke into the air and undid his belt. "I'll disguise myself as one of the nurses, find out what room she's in, and kill her." He thought about it for a moment. That's a damn good plan. Gina is good at disguising herself. He knew she could get the job done. He felt his manhood growing as she worked her hand down his pants. She started to massage his manhood. The pain he felt all over his body vanished. Maybe, it was a mind thing. Gina loves to talk about killing people while having sex. He grabbed her by the ass and squeezed. "Yes, that'll be a great idea. Let's wait two days before we act. I'm sure the doctors will be done with their tests. The police won't come around asking questions to an unresponsive woman. With them out of the way, getting to her shouldn't be much of a problem." He took the cigarette from her and put it out. He pulled her panties to the side and lifted her butt upwards to insert his hard penis. He penetrated her deeply with long strokes. Her moans made him feel invincible to pain. Sex with Gina felt amazing and so would be Kim's death.

Chapter 14
ADVENTURE ROAD -KANE-

We finally left the hospital. It was hard to leave Kim alone. I had a lot on my mind. Walking back to the car felt longer than expected. Rick informed me of new information to consider. My father had another occupation. He used to go on business trips under a different alias, Bill Right. What the hell was he trying to hide? The agent said he made large transactions and some were not able to be unidentified. The information hit me like a tidal wave. What shocked me the most was the guy who got killed in the accident. His partner is on the run. Kim didn't give up without a fight. I'm proud of her. I'm glad she stabbed that bastard in the neck. He deserved to die. We left the hospital and I thanked the lady at the desk again before we walked out. For some reason, I felt like someone was following me. I scanned the parking lot. Nobody was there. Maybe, it's my time. Smoke popped the locks on the door and we got in. I leaned the seat back to relax my mind. I felt under a lot of stress, but I'm not about to give up on myself. I decided to take back control. When I got released from jail, since then it seems as if something took command of my life. I have to turn things around before it gets worse. My brother is a maniac, my father was murdered and had a secret identity. My mom is in a mental hospital and Kim is in a coma. Smoke put his head down in his hands. I heard him crying. Damn, what happened to Kim had to be just as hard on him. His emotions were the same as mine. I know Smoke loves Kim in a sister kind of way. They grew up together. We became best friend and she became his sister. He felt like family should always stick together. I remember he had said that when we were on the track field. Now, the pressure is getting to him. His grandmother and Kim. A world of misfortune all crumbling down. I placed my hand on his shoulder. "Smoke... it's going to be alright." I whispered. "Kim will make it through this. She's a fighter." He looked up from his hands and sniffed a few times. "I can't believe what happened to her. The nicest person anyone could ever meet... and that happened to her. They raped her and now she's in a coma." "I know man." I whispered. "It's fucked up what happened. We have to find the guy who did this and kill him." Smoke put the car in drive and pulled away from the hospital. We got on the highway heading down 85 South. We were both quiet. I thought about Kim. Then, I thought about my father and what Rick said about him. I watched the city through the passenger window. It was beautiful. I tapped Smoke on the dashboard and pointed towards the Pleasant Hill exit. He looked confused because my exit is three down. I told him to stop at my father's office. He got off and we pulled up to the building. "Wait here, I'll be right back." "Kane, what's going on? The place looks closed down." I got out of the car and shut the door. I looked through the window. "It is, but I need you to trust me on this one. I need you to watch out for me, cool? I know how to get in. Just give me ten minutes. If the cops show, blow the horn." He agreed and I made my way to the back of the building. I checked the door, it was locked. I stepped back to a line of bricks around the flower garden. I counted to the sixteenth brick in line and removed it. Bingo. I grabbed the key. Hopefully, they didn't change the lock. I put the key in and turned. A clicking sound was a notification that the key my father hid still worked. I entered the office and turned on the light switch. They flickered on before brightening the room. The place looked the same but covered in dust. My answer is somewhere in here. I searched the front for anything I could find while making my way to the main office. I walked through the door and immediately felt my father's presence guiding me to the answer. I searched his desk and then the closet. I couldn't find anything useful. There had to be something here. I felt around the closet. I placed my hands on the wall. It felt hollow. Suddenly, the back wall slid sideways and revealed an empty safe. Whatever my father hid inside got him killed. There's a possibility it was a hit on Jar Simmons, not Bill Right.

Chapter 15
MAN OF HONOR -JORDAN-

I've been in the office lately and Rick has been out in the field. He's doing well by providing me with good information. The last couple of days had been hectic. Especially, around the here. It's been pure mayhem. The girlfriend of Kane Simmons was kidnapped. Everything about this kid is bad news. My desk is covered with paperwork and pictures of crime scenes. I'm backed up with work just from their family. I'm mentally and physically tired of being at the office. My mind started to play tricks on me. I need to be in the field with Rick chasing bad guys. Kane puts down a vicious hitman the FBI had been trying to track down for the past couple of years. Ke'Mo Cut was not a pushover at the least. Hell, I worked undercover in the same room with that monster. His twisted mind was nothing nice. I studied the crime scene photos and it didn't end well for Ke'Mo. A BMW was shot up and he took a bullet to the head. Judging by the photos. Kane might have had the guts to kill this guy. The bullet to the head was a suicide blow if you ask me. Guys like Ke'Mo take pride in their work. He would never let a punk like Kane end his life. The gun on the scene was found in his hand. We're waiting for the results to find out if there were different fingerprints on the murder weapon. Kane prints will come back if he committed the crime. It doesn't matter to the director if he murdered Ke'Mo. The case will never make it to trial. It's more like we want to know for ourselves, who knocked off the great Ke'Mo Cut. Some of the guys even placed bets if he did it or not. I ran through most of the reports and finished finalizing all of my paperwork. I checked my watch. It was 9:18 am when Rick approached my desk the right way without me having to put a bullet in his ass for creeping up behind me. He finally got that part right. He sat down. "Hey, what's going on? I brought some coffee." He handed me a cup. I smelt the steam coming from the coffee. I don't like open drinks brought to me. That kind of scares the shit out of me, especially when I was undercover. I saw a few guys drop that way, poison slipped into their drinks. I guess the thought of dying that way bothers me. I placed the cup on my desk. When I finish with Rick, I'll go to the restroom and dump it. "Thanks, Rick." I gave him a fake smile. "I'm just finishing the last bit of paperwork. It's stressful sitting around here all day.

I can't lie about that. What's up with you? You have anything new for me?" Rick sipped his coffee. "Well, as a matter of fact, I do. I was at the hospital yesterday doing a check up on the victim from the kidnapping. Turns out, when I got there I couldn't speak with her." I looked at Rick confused as he continued. "The accident put her in a coma. It's a very sad situation. I can't imagine my daughter being in a coma. Anyway, I stuck around for a moment to talk to the doctor. Funny coincidence because we were friends in high school. After catching up with him, guess who shows up?" I don't give a damn about him being high school butt buddies with some doctor. I want him to stop prolonging the damn story and get to the point. I need to get the hell out of the office. Sitting here listening to Rick's fieldwork adventures made me sick to my stomach. I should be the one out there putting in work, but no. The Director of the FBI ordered my crazy ass to stay off the streets. I was undercover for too long, according to him. I need to lay low for a while or whatever that meant. Well, I'm tired of this lay low shit. Rick continued. "That's right, our boy. When I wrapped up my report on the girl. I was about to call it a night. Kane Simmons walked right through the door. He told the doctor he was the girl's husband. Which you and I both know they're not married. Before I introduced myself, he got very emotional. The entire scene completely blew me away. I used the opportunity to get some information from him. I tried to gain his trust a little by telling him about Ke'Mo Cut. You should've seen the look on his face. He did answer a few questions. Nothing we don't know already. After that, I left and waited in the parking lot to tail him. He went to his father's office, I don't have a solid reason why, but... we got him."

Chapter 16
MIND GAMES -KANE-

I woke up the next morning for the second time without Kim. That's something I was not ready to get comfortable with. I got up from the bed and walked into the bathroom to wash my face with cold water. Man, I felt disoriented for some reason. I wrung out the rag and wiped my face. After I finished I looked in the mirror. Fuck! My father appeared out of nowhere. I jumped back taken by surprise. I kept my eyes glued to the mirror. I heard my father say, "Home." I took a step towards the mirror. He vanished when I tried to touch his face on the glass. Instead, I felt a jolt through my entire body and I was back in the bed. Fuck! It was a dream. I woke up in a cold sweat. It seemed real. I sat up in the bed, breathing heavily as I contemplated what just happened. The dream made my body feel tense. I don't believe in ghosts and shit like that, but I do believe my father just tried to tell me something. I heard him say, home. My mind was tripping. Some people say if you think about something before you go to bed you'll dream about it. Before I fell asleep, I thought about my father and the empty safe. That was the only thing on my mind. Damn, shit was getting crazy. I got up and went into the bathroom. I turned on the cold water to wash my face for real this time. I checked the mirror just to make sure I wasn't insane. My father didn't appear in the mirror. I grabbed the rag and soap. I washed my face. When I was finished, the whole situation felt like déjà vu. I slowly removed the rag from my face the exact way as the last time. I peered into the mirror before I fully removed it this time. Good, I still had some sense. No ghost father sending subliminal messages. I finished in the bathroom and went into the closet. I dressed in the clothes Kim bought for me when I first got out. It'll be mandatory to see her every single day. I know she'll pull through this, I need her. We were meant to be together. Smoke is on the way to pick me up. I heard my phone go off. Damn, he's here already? I know he's fast but damn. That's quick. I left the closet and grabbed the pants I wore yesterday. Unknown caller, it's wasn't him. I answered, "This Kane." "How is she?" It was a familiar voice. The Planner. I got so caught up with everything else that I forgot about my deal with this maniac. Something inside of me returned. That surge of adrenaline, that rage of another person began to take control. Maybe because I'm not fully certain if he had something to do with Kim's kidnapping. Just mentioning something about her somehow savagely pissed me off. "Don't you worry about how she's doing." I said sternly. "Just worry about what we have going on. I'm tired of bullshittin' with you. You got the money or not?" He was quiet for a moment before speaking. "Well, well, well. Somebody's pissed off. Is that any kind of way to talk to the person who found her? You should appreciate my concern." He started laughing. It sounded wicked and harsh behind the static. "Now, my diamond. That's what actually matters to me. The deal is now four million, correct?" I didn't answer. I felt like snatching his ass through the phone and beating him to death. Talking about Kim infuriated me. "I'm positive you agree with that. Make sure you follow directions carefully this time around. I'm trying to avoid getting someone killed. I can't lose any more men. It's bad for business. You know good help is extremely hard to find these days. I want you at the phone booth on the corner of-" "No, fuck that!" I interrupted. "You listen to me. I have the diamond and I don't feel safe following your plans. My friend and I almost got killed. We will meet where I want to meet. If this deal is to go down, it will be the way I want it to happen. You sent a damn hitman last time. That's right, I know about Ke'Mo Cut. That was some real ho shit you pulled. I'm lucky to still be alive. If something like that happens again, you can forget about the diamond. I'll sell it to someone else. Hell, just to make sure you don't get it. I'll throw the damn thing in the ocean." "Ok, what do you suggest?" "Give me three days to get myself together. I need time to clear my head. Call me and I'll have the details then." I hung up the phone just like that. I didn't give him time to respond. I took a chance on losing the deal. I don't care. I'm tired of being controlled. I'm controlling things now and that's the way it's going to be from here on out. I have to come up with a damn good plan in three days. I know he'll call back and I'll be prepared for him. I still have other things to take care of. I'm running the show and I got a plan for The Planner.

Chapter 17
CALL ME A SAINT

The Planner was furious about having to wait three days to get the diamond. No doubt the game was on. Kane had a behavior change. Kids these days, he thought. Everybody wants to be in love. He wouldn't give two cents to bring his girlfriend out of the coma. Drama fueled his soul and he wanted Kane to suffer. He even prayed for her not to survive. He couldn't help but smile while thinking about it. He felt great today. There's no other option, but to patiently wait three days. Until then, he had to find something to occupy his evil mind. The first thing he planned to do was call his connect, The Buyer. The man who originally sought after the African Black Diamond. He met the African two years ago when the diamond was first brought to the museum. The Buyer offered him fifty million dollars to steal it. The Africans knew they couldn't get the diamond back to their country without a war. They were ready to travel to purchase it in person. He planned to ask The Buyer for three more days to get the stone. The Planner was skeptical about what Kane will demand. He would resort to plan B if the situation doesn't work in his favor. That meant Kane would have to die at a later time. He made a smart decision when he threatened to destroy his dream of possessing the diamond. That would ruin his deal with the Africans. And they were crazy enough to travel over just to slaughter him for bad business. He had to capitalize on having the money arrive at the same time as the diamond. Kane and The Buyer would have to meet him at the same location. Four million dollars would have to be put in a separate suitcase. The Buyer would receive the diamond and take his ass back to Africa. Then he would reluctantly give Kane his share of the money. Just in case the situation got out of line. He set his mind on sending someone in his place. He smiled because another body on his behalf would be risky. No one could be left alive who knew his identity. That's the way I roll baby. Kill or be killed. He stopped at a payphone and placed a collect call. The Buyer's assistant accepted the call then directed it to his office. "Yes, my friend?" He said in a strong African accent. "Do you have what my hard-earned money is paying you for?" Rich sonofvabitch, he thought. I can't see how it's hard-earned money when crazy motherfuckers from the jungle kill for it on your behalf. "I'll have the diamond in three days. I need four million in a separate suitcase. The diamond will be yours without any hassle. I went ahead and booked a room at a hotel in Atlanta for your stay under a private name. I'll send you the information. No one will ever know you were in the states. I'll meet you there. The diamond will arrive shortly after. "If something goes wrong. I'm sure you know the punishment is death. And trust me... That's the nicest thing I can offer. Three days, expect my arrival." He hung up. The Planner is cold-hearted, but the Africans were black-hearted. Hell, they didn't have one. There's no telling what they would do to him if something doesn't go according to plan. This deal must go smoothly. He heard stories about the African man known as The Buyer. He had figured out he's the General of the almighty African Army. A group of savages under his control that uses brutal force on those who oppose the law. He walked away from the phone booth, thinking about what to do next. He had to relieve unwanted tension that built up throughout his body. He grabbed his pistol inside his overcoat. I should go to the hospital and kill Kane's girlfriend. Nah, too much heat. He looked up and down the block for a potential victim. Everyone moved freely in their own world. He hated it. People thought nothing bad would ever happen to them. Which one to choose, there's so many of them. He wished he had brought his Ak-47 from the house and let open fire decide who die. He pulled the gun from his overcoat and aimed toward the sky. Funny, people were so busy that they failed to notice a crazy man with the gun. He fired several shots into the air. Pandemonium broke out and cause civilians to panic. He ducked off in a nearby coffee shop. He watched through the window as people ran for their lives in fear. "What's going on?" The man stood behind the front counter. "Oh, nothing." The Planner turned around and smirked. "I just woke a few people up."

Chapter 18
AROUND THE CLOCK -KANE-

After I finished getting myself together, I got a bite to eat. Smoke should pull up any minute. I'm on the way to visit my mother and then Kim. For the last few days, I felt bad about everything in my life. Since I talked to The Planner I've gained an unfamiliar surge of confidence. My life is about to turn around for the better. I thought about the empty safe hidden behind the wall in the closet. Somebody murdered my father because of what it contained inside, I felt it. He would never leave something that important unsecured around the house. I don't remember him being sloppy to that extent. In the case of the left open safe. Why hide it behind a wall if you're that careless? I have to investigate some more but now is not the time. After my visits are over I'll get back to business. I went back into the closet and peeled off five hundred dollars from my bankroll. I couldn't forget about the people I care about in my life. This money is for my boy, T-Mac. Hopefully, it'll be enough to help him cool out for a minute. I know he's having a hard time not having anyone to send money. I'm thankful to have good friends who care enough about my well-being. My phone started ringing and I answered. "Smoke, I'm on the way down." "Cool." He said nonchalantly. I got everything I needed and locked up. I opened the door and got in the car. I gave my boy some dap. "Sup, feeling any better? I appreciate what you're doing for me." I strapped on my seat belt and adjusted the seat back as usual. "I'm good, thanks for your concern." He sounded a bit better than before. "Don't worry about it, you're my boy. I'll take you around the world and back. Plus, Kim's like a sister to me. I have to check on her or she'll be mad. You know how she'll get if she found out I didn't check-in. She'll put me in a coma." He started up the car. "Forget about me, everything straight with you?" "I'm good. Just spending time with them will make me feel a whole lot better. I got another call from The Planner." I told him straight up. He looked at me with wide eyes. "What did he say? I hope he doesn't think we forgot about that little confrontation with that Ke'Mo guy. This time we need to be ready for some shit like that." "That's the first thing I took care of. I told him, I'm calling all the shots from here on out. I have three days to come up with a full proof plan to get the money without getting us killed. When he calls, I'll be ready." Smoke reversed the car out of the parking lot. "Where to first?" "The gas station. I need to pick up a money order. After that, Hill Heights and then... the hospital." I whispered the last part. It hurt just thinking about Kim's condition. We left the neighborhood and drove to the gas station up the block. I ran in real quick and got a five hundred dollar money order for T-Mac. Afterward, we hurried over to Hill Heights. I went in and Smoke waited for me in the car. I walked into the building and signed-in. No other visits were for my mother, just me. The situation was sad. I was led outside to my mother. She was seated in her usual spot by the rose bush. I walked over and pulled up a chair. She looked beautiful. One of the nurses did her hair and put make-up on her face. That was a kind thing to do. At least they care about how she looked. I faced her and spoke. "Mom, I went to visit my father's office the other day and... I found a safe hidden in the closet behind the back wall. I believe he was murdered for whatever was inside. I wish you would talk to me because there are some questions I need you to answer. When he left the country, he used a different alias." I looked at my mother to see if she would show any signs of emotion. None, she just focused on the rose bush. I continued. "The name he used was Bill Right. I met an FBI agent name, Rick Chase. He told me everything and seemed convincing when he spoke. He's helping solve the murder investigation. I had a dream last night that my father came to visit me. I'm trying to find out what it meant. It's been a lot of things going wrong in my life. Kim was kidnapped and raped. Now she's at Grady Hospital in a coma after being in a bad accident with the kidnappers. Do you remember Kim? She's the only woman I ever brought home. Remember when you both cooked for everyone on Thanksgiving? I don't know what I'll do without her. I already lost my father and from that, you. I'm trying my best to hold myself together. Before I leave, there's something I have to tell you and I hope one day you'll understand. That day the police arrested me for murder. I promise you I didn't have anything to do with it. It was... Abel. Mother, he murdered the teacher. I thought I would take the secret to the grave. Now... you know the truth."

Chapter 19

SMOKE DETECTOR

I got back to the car and tapped on the window. Smoke had adjusted his seat all the way back and propped his feet out of the driver's side window. He was knocked out cold. "Yo, Smoke... unlock the door? He woke up and let me in. "Damn, talking about being out for the count. If I didn't get here on time, one of these old women would've taken advantage of you." I joked and got in the car. "Aye, the way I'm feelin' right now I would've invited it." He laughed. "Yeah, I bet you would enjoy it." He shrugged his shoulders and started up the car. We talked a little about my visit with my mother. Mainly about how she was doing and her well-being. I kept personal information to myself. I could've told Smoke about my brother, but now wasn't the time. One day when all this drama clears out, I'll let him know. That's my boy and I can tell him anything, but something like this I rather keep to myself. My father said keep your friends close and your enemies closer. Well, Smoke is without a doubt my best friend, but The Planner is in my pocket. I had to change things around on him. Instead of being hit with blind calls. I have him where I want him and he knows it. We turned onto 85 south heading towards Atlanta. I felt the need to tell Smoke about my dream. There's a possibility he might be able to figure out what it meant. I don't know, maybe? "Man, let me tell you about this crazy dream I had." "Oh, yeah." He turned down the music. "What's up?" "My father," I saw the look of concern on his face. He probably thought I was about to lay a sad story on him. Smoke care about my feelings like a brother. He knew how close I was with my father and how fragile my mind get whenever mentioning him. "Your pops?" He asked. "Yeah... He paid me a visit while I was asleep. The shit seemed real. I woke up and walked into the bathroom and started washing my face. When I removed the rag he appeared in the mirror. I jumped back a little shook. I thought I had lost my mind. I heard him say, home. I tried to touch the mirror to see if my eyes were telling the truth. My mother already lost her sanity and I thought what happened to her could happen to me. His face became a blur and the image vanished. A shock wave went through my body and I woke up in a cold sweat. I couldn't feel anything as I walked back into the bathroom. I tried to recreate the scene the exact way as last time. Nothing happened. I thought about it a few times and still can't figure it out. He tried to tell me something, but what? He just said, home." I looked at Smoke and he seemed to be trying to decipher the dream in his head. "Well, I believe he wants you to go back home. But that could be something you haven't accomplished. Meaning, bring your mother home. You might find something at the crib that he wants you to have. I'm throwing this out there, a message sent from Heaven to let you know he's safe at home. Who knows? Whatever your heart tells you is probably the right answer. It's for you to decide." I would have told him in the same manner if it were him. He had a valid point about listening to my heart. I do feel a certain way about it that I can't quite explain, but I know what it is. "Thanks, man. I needed somebody else to tell me I wasn't losing my mind." "No problem," He said. "You would've done the same for me." We pulled into the hospital. We signed in and didn't have to wait that long. We went directly to Kim's room. I walked through the door and she was in the same position. The doctor from before stood next to her. He watched him scribble a few notes on a small pad. Hopefully, it's good news. Smoke took a seat in one of the chairs. The doctor greeted us as we approached. I don't think he expected us to sneak up. He answered a few of my questions before he left the room. She didn't get any better. This shit is beginning to beat me up inside. I sat next to the bed and held my head in her left hand and did the only thing I could do to help her. I prayed.

Chapter 20
THE GANG

We left the hospital after about two hours. I rather spend life behind bars than see Kim in a coma for that long. Just knowing she was going to be alright and safe would be fine with me. I have to get what happened out of my mind. I won't let my emotions get the best of me right now. I have to take what I'm about to plan seriously without any distractions. In just two days The Planner will call. I have to be ready and not just for a swap. I have to expect a war. On the way back to the apartment I made a call to Bear and Redd. I will need all the help I can get on this one. My friends will have my back and friend is a very strong word, but they're golden. They were down to rob a bank and pull off a heist. We stole the world's most expensive diamond. Now, tell me they're not my boys? Before all of this mess came about, I was in a cage for two years. They were the only people who came to visit me in that hell hole. That's one of the main reasons I call them my friends. Every opportunity they got to put money on my books, they did. Even when they couldn't afford it. They needed it more than me. My father took care of that easily, but they still insisted. I can call on them for anything and this was one of those times. If I'm getting into an all-out war with this Planner psychopath. I'll need friends who are willing to die for me just like I would for them. End of story. I have to orchestrate the perfect game plan so nobody gets killed. It's boiling down to the end game and it's about to get hectic. We pulled into the neighborhood. I unlocked the apartment door and went straight into the kitchen to pour myself a shot of vodka. A clear mind helps to start a good thinking process. Smoke walked into the kitchen and ordered a shot. I poured one for him and had a second for myself. My phone rang, it was Redd. He let me know they were on the way up to the door. I told him it was unlocked. Three minutes later, they came through and we greeted each other as if we were family. They noticed the shot glasses on the table next to Smoke. Of course, they placed an order. Before you know it, we were tipsy. I kept the shots rolling. A bunch of shit ran around in my mind. Just relaxing for a change with my boys made things feel better. We settled in the living room and chopped it up for a moment. We talked about old times and how fun school use to be. Smoke and I won state titles. The YouTube video Redd and

I created that went viral. Our basketball team was great that year. If I didn't go to jail, we could've won a championship. We were ranked number one in the state newspaper. Bear and I had a good run while playing football. I believe if I had the chance to play my junior year. We would've brought that guy home. I felt good that they were around. Real friends, I could talk to rather than think about all the bad shit that happened in my life. Smoke fired up a blunt full of Kush and everyone hit it. I choked a little because I only smoked two times in my entire life and still wasn't used to it. It felt good though, very relaxing. I quietly sat there for a moment, listening to them talk about the past. The Kush had my mind blown and I really couldn't focus on everything at once. I drifted into a world of my own. I focused on one subject before traveling to the next. I leaned back in my chair and zoned out. I felt like everyone else in the room vanished and I was all alone. I thought about what Rick said about my father. I remained mentally focused on that for ten minutes, to what I discovered in the closet. The safe. What the hell was in it? Knowing my father it would be hard to tell. I tried to remember things I saw him with that he valued. I should know the answer to this without any problem. As many times I've been in the office, you would think it should be a no brainer. He did hold a secret from me. In which I truly believe he sent me a message regarding, home. I thought long and hard about it. Home?

Maybe, the answer to the message is at my house? I can't just show up with Abel there, he has a restraining order on me. I guess it's time for another break-in. I spoke up. "Yo, I have a plan."

Chapter 21
COMMIT TO DEATH

After going over the entire plan with my boys, we all agreed that it was full proof. We spent the afternoon advising and revising it until we felt it was perfect. Our lives were on the line. The last time I dealt with The Planner, he almost put me and Smoke in a casket. This time things will be different. Redd and Bear said their goodbye's and called it a night. It was only seven o'clock and I wanted to grab a bite to eat. I offered to pay Smoke if he drove me to the nearest soul food spot. He agreed and we left the apartment. On the way to the restaurant, I saw the store my father used to buy all of my mother's jewelry. The place was closed for the evening. I wanted to get a gift for Kim. I'll stop by after we finish getting our food and find out what time they open tomorrow. We made it to the soul food spot and I ordered enough food for a family of apes. Smoke didn't get much. We left heading back to the jewelry store. I got out and approached the door. The sign said, 8 am until 7 pm. We just missed it. I hopped back in the car and told Smoke the time and we peeled out. He'll stop by tomorrow an hour early so I'll have time to get something special for my lady. We pulled into my apartment complex. I gave Smoke some dap before I got out and told him to drive home safe. I don't want anything to happen to my best friend with all the stuff that's been going down. Who knows, shit happens. I entered the apartment. I instantly felt lonely without Kim. I smashed the food fast as I could to keep my mind from wondering about anything else. After I finished, I took a long hot shower and went to bed. Hopefully, my father will visit in my sleep again. I got up the next morning and immediately thought day two. One more day before I meet The Planner. I looked at the alarm clock. Right on time, seven o'clock. An hour before the jewelry store opens. Smoke will be here around eight to pick me up for my normal runs. After I washed my face and brushed my teeth, I put on something nice for the day. Man, I got some good sleep. The best I had in a long time. I haven't been able to sleep after what happened to Kim. Smoke called and said he was waiting in his normal parking spot. I grabbed a few things from the closet before I left. One was five thousand dollars. I want to buy Kim an engagement ring. If I die in the next few days. I want her to wake up with a ring on her finger. She needs to know how much I love her. I hopped in the ride and pounded up my boy Smoke before strapping on the seat belt. We pulled out and headed over to the jewelry store. "Yo, I decided what I want to get Kim." I was sincere when I spoke. "Oh," He sounded intrigued. "What are you thinking about?" "I want to get her a ring." I just came out with it to see the response on his face. "One day when this is all over, I want us to get married." "Really," He said with a bright smile. "I think that's a wonderful idea." "When she wakes up I want to propose to her. I love her that much. I was thinking about the last few days that if something happens to me, I want her to know. You know the type of shit we're about to get into is dangerous as hell." We drove into the jewelry store parking lot. "Well, as her big brother you have my consent." He had a serious look on his face while holding out his hand. I smiled and we shook hands like men. We got out and walked into the store. When we got inside, I recognized the Indian man behind the front counter. I walked up to him. "Hey, how are you today, sir. Do you remember me?" He looked at me kind of funny. "I'm Jar's son." I smiled as I told him. "Mr. Simmons, son?" He was shocked. "Man, oh man. You've grown. I remember when your father... " He paused and put his head down. "It's ok, I'm good now." I assured him. "I heard the news and I'm sorry for what happened to your family." "Thanks, I appreciate your gratitude." I said. "I'm here to find a ring for a very special woman." He smiled. "Becoming a man, I see. Come, come, I'll show you." He showed me some beautiful engagement rings. Finally, after about thirty minutes I picked one. I spent four thousand. The ring was $8,000 and he gave me half off because of the friendship he had with my father. I thanked him. I got to the door and turned around. I almost forgot about the other thing I came for. I held out a brochure. "Hey, my friend, can you make this?" We left the jewelry store and made our way over to Kim. Man, I felt good. I won't stop praying for her to make it. I want her to be fully recovered when I say those words. Will you marry me? That's a big step, but I'm ready to commit to her for the rest of my life. Smoke started the car. I pulled the ring out and stared at it. The damn thing was immaculate. My parents would be proud of me. They're big on marriage. Smoke glanced at it. "I'm proud of you, man. If my sister is to marry someone. I'm happy it's you. I know you're the only person she loves like that. I knew it the first day she talked about you. That's why I hooked you up with her." "Thanks, she's the one for me." We arrived at the hospital. We went up to Kim's room and settled in. The doctor wasn't present. Smoke took a seat at the other end of the room by the TV. He wanted to show some respect by giving us some privacy. I pulled up a seat next to the bed and I grabbed her hand. I closed my eyes and held my head up high this time. I mean every word that I'm about to speak from my mouth. "Kim..." I whispered. "The first thing I want to say is that I love you. My heart told me you're the one. Since the first day we met. I never loved another woman before in my life besides my mother. I know deep down in my heart you love me the same. I feel that somewhere in the dream world you're in, you can hear me and understand what I'm saying. You have always been there and I appreciate everything you have ever done. I'm more than glad you entered my life. I don't know how to explain what I'll do if I lose you. I miss you so much and can't imagine ever being without you. Words can't explain how much I love you. I want to marry you. I bought this ring for you to show how much I care about our relationship." I slipped the ring on her finger and kissed her hand. I put the card I bought for her on the stand next to the bed. I wrote on the inside I love you and will you marry me. Just in case I don't make it back to tell her. It'll explain everything. I got up and went over to Smoke. "Yo, I'm about to run down to the food court and grab a bite to eat." "Cool, I'm coming too." He stood. "I can use something to snack on." We left the room, heading to the food court. I bought a hamburger and some fries. Smoke stared at the list on the menu board like he was a kid again. He finally decided after five minutes of gawking at the display photos. We made our way back to the room. We exited the elevator to the second floor. One of the nurses waved at me as she went by and stepped in the elevator. Damn, she looked familiar. I stopped and turned around to catch a second glimpse of her right before the elevator closed. Smoke did the same and stared at me with a confused look on his face. "Yo, you want to get married, remember?" Her haircut and eyes were very familiar. "Nah, it's not that. That woman, it's something about her. I saw her somewhere before." "You sure? She does work here. Maybe you caught her in a different section in the hospital." He suggested. I shook my head while slowly turning back around. "I don't think so. Not here, in another place." He shrugged and we continued walking to Kim's room. Suddenly, I froze. I remembered where I knew her from. The museum! "Shit!" I dropped the food right there in the hall and gunned it to Kim. I slid to a stop in front of the room barely able to slow down. I threw open the door. She was alright. At least she appeared to be fine. Smoke flew in behind me. I still felt something was wrong. I hurried over to her and started unhooking shit. Smoke looked frantic, but he helped. My instincts told me to get her out of the room immediately. We pushed the bed into the hallway. The third room down was unoccupied. We rolled her in safely. I felt better after she was out of the room. I told Smoke to watch over her. I had to go back to get the card I bought with the ring. I put my hand on the knob and suddenly the room exploded. The force propelled me into the air and I collided against the back wall. I grabbed my chest while watching the room engulfed in flames.

Chapter 22
BE COOL

My back was in an excruciating amount of pain. I heard the alarm sound. I couldn't see anything in the room. Everything got covered in flames. Black smoke filled my lungs and I began to choke to death. I had to pick myself up and go after the woman. I slowly gained the strength to get up. I staggered forward leaning against the wall. In only four steps I stopped, feeling disoriented. After I regained my balance, I took flight like a jet. I repeatedly punched the button on the elevator. It wasn't moving fast enough for me. By the time it open, she would've escaped. I looked to my right, recalling the entrance to the stairs. I hurried over and slung open the door. I held the rail for support and descended five steps at a time. I cleared the last seven stairs without a problem. "One hundred hall." I read the sign on the door as I rounded the staircase to the next set of steps. I cleared them. "Main Floor." I read the next sign pinned to the door as I pushed through the exit. I shot a glance over to the elevators. Nothing. The woman had to be somewhere in the parking lot. I swiftly scanned the lower level as I made my way over to the exit. I made sure I didn't past her on the way. She was nowhere to be found. I went through the automatic door and emerged in the hospital's main parking garage. I scanned the scene as if I possessed hawk eyes. Found her. She was on the far left end of the lot. I took off at track speed. She was really on the move and hurried to get inside her car. I felt like I wouldn't catch her. I ran fast as I could and tried to move even faster. Somewhere down in my legs I felt a sense of urgency and began to gain even more speed. I wanted to catch this demon woman. She tried to blow up a room in an attempt to murder Kim. Suddenly, her car back out and burnt out towards the entrance. I closed in and made a death-defying leap onto the vehicle. I made it by the grace of God. I felt the woman swerving the car back and forth trying to throw me off. I've never done anything suicidal in my life, not counting my last few criminal activities I've been involved in. This made me feel like a stuntman in an action movie. My hands held onto the ends of the back windshield. I made sure I had a firm grip because getting thrown from a moving vehicle would be horrible. I don't give a damn and wasn't thinking about it too tough. I had to catch this woman. I cautiously crawled up the back end of the car onto the roof. She was driving wildly through the parking lot. Bull riders need to start practicing like this. I promise I would've won first place in one of those contests. The car continued to swerve back and forth violently as I positioned on the roof. I don't know what I'm doing or what my next move will be. I rubbed my hand across the driver's side window liner. The window was down. Good, maybe I could reach inside and force her to stop the vehicle. I blindly stuck my hand inside the car. I felt cloth-like material and heard the woman yell, get your filthy hands off me! That's when I knew I had her. I took hold of the cloth with a firm grip. I started to yank the shit out of it, trying to throw her off track. She started yelling and swearing to let her go. That's when a loud boom erupted. I thought for a moment she wrecked the car. I was still alive and the vehicle continued to maneuver around the lot. The wind blew my dreads back wildly let me know we were on the move. I heard the sound several more times. Boom, boom, boom! Damn, she had a gun and was shooting through the roof. I saw bullet holes form like little metal volcanoes on the passenger side. I threw off her aim by jerking her. I was scared for my life so I started yanking her harder than before. All of a sudden, the car came to a harsh stop. I felt my body reluctantly slide off the roof. I was thrown forward and violently hit the pavement and came to a rolling stop. I spit dirt and blood from my mouth. I slowly pick myself up from the ground. I was taken by surprise when the woman gunned the car in my direction. I leaped to safety almost being struck by the vehicle. I jumped back to my feet. The woman sped from the hospital parking lot. She got away. "Damn."

Chapter 23
MY MOTHER'S SEED

After the death threat on my life, I made my way back into the hospital. There was commotion throughout the two hundred hallway. I waited around for a moment until the police arrived. Plus, I want to make sure Kim is safe. Finally, the fire department arrived first on the scene. They went to work and then the police showed. I answered a few questions and let them know the suspect is a woman. I never told them about our encounter at the museum. I kept that bit of information to myself. They had me look through staff pictures of women employed at the hospital. Not even one matched my description. I made it look good even though I knew she wasn't an employee at the hospital. One of the officers scribbled down a few notes. They even called me a hero. The boy who saved his girlfriend from a museum thief. That's kind of what I thought about it. Smoke told them what he knew. I thought it was a good thing he kept it short and sweet, the less the better. I knew Kim was safe so I decided to get ghost, too many police officers for me. I've been involved in a bank robbery and a museum heist. Not to mention a couple of Wild Wild West shootouts. Anxiety started to build and that made me want to vanish from the scene. Someone might try to start up a quiz show and I'm not sticking around to be a contestant. I'm out of here, you better believe it. I signed at Smoke. He immediately picked up on what I was trying to say. We got the hell out of that cop infested cesspool. I got in the car and let out a sigh of relief. My body was exhausted from everything that just took place. Kim is still alive and I didn't get killed by that psycho. What the hell is with that woman? All I could think about was how did she know about Kim? The situation grabbed my mind in a stranglehold and twisted my thoughts. I really want to know who she is. She found out about me without any problem and attacked the woman I love. Did The Planner send her for the way I spoke to him on the phone? I thought about that for a moment. Why would he do something like that a day before we are supposed to meet? That's crazy. I don't think he would try me like that after I threatened him. This woman is probably working with someone, but not with him. Someone opened fire on us from the vent that assisted her escape. I thought she fled that scene scared of what could happen. She knew her chances of obtaining the diamond was low. Therefore, she possibly followed us back to the apartment. Damn, how stupid of me. She could've been watching us while plotting to get the diamond with her team. I thought about my mother. If she followed me to Hill Heights. Shit! My mother could be in danger. I told Smoke to gun it to the mental hospital. I explained to him what I thought could have happened and he had no problem picking up the pace. We made it there in record time. I jumped out and ran through the front doors. I checked the sign-in sheet for my mother. There were no other visits. I ask the woman at the front desk was my mother alright and that I've been really worried about her. I got a little hysterical and had to calm down so I wouldn't scare anybody. She called the nurses station in the back where my mother is being kept. They said she was out spending time in the yard. I checked the clock on the wall. She's usually out there around this time. Just hearing that made me feel a whole lot better. I asked if my mother could be relocated to another room for safety reasons and if her visitation name could be changed. She made it happen and I thanked her for being helpful. I finished speaking with the woman at the desk. I made my way out to the yard. My mother looked better than ever. I spotted her in front of her normal spot at the rose bush. I pulled up a chair and kissed her on the forehead before I sat down. Damn, it felt good to know she's fine. I wanted to guard her with my life and stay at the hospital all night on watch, but I couldn't. You can only visit for two hours a day until patients are close to recovering or preparing for departure. I didn't know what to say to my mother at the time. I just bent my head down close to her and I started crying. I broke down for a moment. Suddenly, I felt a hand rest on my head. I looked up and it was hers. She moved. I was astonished because she hadn't lifted a finger towards me since I've been visiting. Even though her attention focused on the rose bush, I felt good about it. She still wouldn't answer or show any signs of emotion, but she moved. That's a sign of hope. I crouched down beside the bush. I wanted to pick a rose from the root and take it back to the room for her. All of them were beautiful. I chose the red one she had her eyes on. I noticed something peculiar under the bush in a patch of dirt. I dug it up and blew it off. It looked like a very expensive ring for a woman. I looked at it skeptically and sat back down in the chair. After gawking at the ring for a moment. I looked over to my mother and was stunned because she stared back at me for the first time since her breakdown.

Chapter 24
THE ARRIVAL

The Buyer sat in his private plane on his way to the states from Africa. The trip would take at least 17 hours. He had everything planned for his arrival. A limousine will be waiting for him and his men. He always planned ahead. His military brain prepared him for the worst outcome in any situation. Precaution is a must. He sent four of his best soldiers to Georgia to settle in immediately after The Planner said the deal would take place in three days ago. The money and weapons were on standby. His relationships with other prominent officials allowed a safe transfer of fifty million dollars and the purchase of assault weapons for his army. They are to be position in a building across from his hotel to stand guard. He ordered two armored Hummers to accompany his bulletproof limousine for protection. Four of his elite bodyguards accompanied him on the plan. Three more hours until he touchdown on a private landing strip outside of Atlanta. The trip was long and he hoped that jet lag wouldn't be harsh after he arrived. His mindset was set on everything working smoothly. The African Black Diamond would be returned home to its original birthplace. The mission was precisely given to him by the African President. He had been ordered to bring the diamond home by any means necessary. There were no limitations on how the mission is supposed to be completed. The diamond is the President's only concern. In his favor, the President is his half-brother which grants him unlimited power. They have been planned to bring the diamond back to Africa since they were young boys. The history behind the diamond means a great deal to them. Africa's leader at the time had ordered their father to command the army against Iraq's assault for the blood diamond. They wanted it and went to battle for their cause. Their stand was successful against Iraq's army. Although, in the line of duty. Their father was brutally murdered, betrayed by one of their own. One of the soldiers shot him in the back of his head while he protected the diamond. The assailant didn't make it far. He got shot in the head by another soldier who stood secretly on guard. The African army lost many men from the battle. As a result, two years later someone stole the diamond. They never figured out how or who committed the crime. The President suspected it had been an inside job. That happened thirty years ago. They just tracked down the diamond in a museum located in Atlanta Georgia two years ago. To avoid a war with the Americans, they found a man to get the job done. The Planner. The Buyer had been offered a hundred million for the diamond to be safely returned and another fifty million dollars in military supplies for his army. The plane finally landed. His men got off first and scanned the scene for a possible threat. They were loyal soldiers and would risk their life without any question. It was clear to transfer to the limo and two armored Hummers that waited at the end of the landing pad. Another four men positioned by their vehicles with AK-47 assault rifles. One of the soldiers waved his hand in the air to sign that the coast was clear. The Buyer got off the plane with his men. They led him to the limo with extreme precaution. He settled in the vehicle. The four elite bodyguards got in with him. His head lieutenant sat in the middle of them. Two soldiers positioned in each Hummer. The vehicles left the private area in an orchestrated manner. The Hummer ahead protected the front and the second held down the back-end. The Buyer looked at the lieutenant. "Is everything in order?" The sound of voice intimidated them. The lieutenant replied. "Yes, General. The money and weapons arrived successfully. We took the position across from the hotel as you ordered." "Good, I'm pleased to hear that everything went smooth as planned. Soon, Africa will get back what is owed to us. If anything happens to any of you while fighting for our cause in battle. The immediate family of fallen soldiers will never worry. Africa will support them for the remainder of their life. You have my word." He raised his glass and gave a toast to each of them simultaneously. "Thank you, General." They showed their generosity at the same time. "To Africa!" The General cheered with a powerful but emotional felt voice. The men echoed his words. "To Africa!" They each took a sip of wine before their leader to check if it had been poisoned. The loyalty, the General snipped the wine before speaking. "To Africa!"

Chapter 25
A STEP AHEAD -KANE-

Yesterday at the mental hospital extremely blew my mind. My mother wasn't staring at the rose bush. She was staring at the spot where she buried her wedding ring. I knew for a fact it belonged to her. After I cleaned it off real good the engraving on the inside read, J.S. & N.S. 4ever. Meaning, Jar Simmons and Noti Simmons forever. My mother must have hidden it when she first arrived at the hospital. I guess she thought it would have been stolen if they noticed it on her finger. She was protecting what she had left of my father. The only problem was trying to put the ring back on her finger. She was persistent with pulling her hand away every time I tried to put the ring on. I figured she was crushed by my father's tragic demise that she couldn't bear to see it. It probably hurt every time she looked at the ring. I finally gave up and put it in my pocket. When she snaps out of it, I'll have it to give back to her.

I got tired. It's going on eight o'clock in the morning. I thought about what my mother had done and all the other stuff I have to get done today. The Planner is at the top of the list, but before I get to him I have something else very important to handle. I've been on a stakeout outside of my house for the last four hours waiting for Abel to leave, so I can break-in. I know he'll leave eventually. He has a problem with staying in one place for a long time. There's got to be something he has to do this wonderful morning. If not, I'll wait. Even if I have to come back every morning. I dragged Smoke along with me. Actually, he wanted to come. My father pointed me towards home. So here I am, waiting to break-in. I don't know what to look for, but it has to be something I forgot about or need to find. That's what I narrowed it down to. I began to doze off. I leaned my seat back to rest, patiently waiting for my brother to appear. My eyes and head got heavy. I caught myself looking at the back of my eyelids a few times. Finally, they were close and I fell asleep. Smoke kept nudging me on the shoulder. I woke up from what was probably a five-minute nap. He kept low as he pointed over to my house. I stayed ducked down in the seat. I looked over and saw Abel, leaving as I expected. Whatever he was doing had to be important because he was with other people. He never had company over before, unless it was a study group or something of the sort. Two other men walked with him. To me, they looked like a group of geeks walking to a science fair. They all got in my mother's Aston Martin. My brother got in the driver seat and the other two men got in the back. I thought that was kind of weird. Suddenly, a woman emerged from the house wearing sunglasses. She fixed her hair while hurrying to the passenger side. My brother has a girlfriend? She had moved fast so I couldn't tell if she was pretty. It's a good thing he has somebody in his life. They finally pulled off and we waited for them to get a good distance away before making a move. I got out and hurried around to the back of the house. I know my key doesn't work, so the front door is not an option. I looked up to my window and knew it was unlocked. When I was younger, I broke the lock on it. When I use to sneak out, I always had a way back in. Nobody knew about it, but me. Not even my father. I guess we do think alike because that was my secret I kept from him. I climbed up the vine tree next to the house and pushed up the window. Open as expected. I climbed through with no problem. I was back in my room. Everything looked the same and untouched. I searched around to make sure I didn't forget anything important. I finished and immediately went to my parent's room. It looked like it had been occupied by someone. The room was a mess and I knew for a fact my parents would never approve. I searched around for a moment and nothing really caught my eye. I stepped towards the door and noticed something peculiar. It was a Yale University yearbook. I walked over and picked it up. I thought about what the detective said, the guy who was in the accident with Kim went to that school. Luckily, my brother is a student there as well. I flipped through a few pages to the name, Alfred Ben. I found every single page he was on and the last one shocked me the most. Alfred was holding hands with Abel and the female from the museum was in the picture with them. I closed the book. It was hard to breathe. I looked down where I found the yearbook and noticed a black notebook with my father's handwriting on the cover. My phone rung. I quickly grabbed the notebook and put everything in a backpack marked... Ali.

Chapter 26
SICK DAY OUT -JORDAN-

I got up and went to work amazingly early. The few people who were in couldn't believe I arrived at that time. I usually get to work around nine or ten in the morning to start the day. Today, I arrived at four in the morning and I've been working my ass off ever since. I wanted to be ahead and knock out every bit of paperwork. I went ahead and made a cup of coffee for myself. I don't want Rick bringing me another death cup. He brought me a cup of Joe every time he came to work and I was getting tired of sneaking to the restroom to dump it. Today, I beat him and I left it half full or half empty. Whatever you want to call it, but I made sure something was in there for him to see and I wouldn't need a refill. I have papers all over my desk from rummaging through files. Getting the job done, I might add. Not the kind of job I want to do, but it pays the bills. I would rather be out in the field getting down and dirty, going undercover on a drug lord or some kind of mafia don. I love danger. This paperwork stuff is taking me out of my element. I hope I don't have field rust from being out of action for so long. Rick wasn't doing all that good of a job. He's been working here for quite some time. Since he has been here, I can't recall him killing or even shooting anybody, shit. I don't believe he drew his gun one time. The West Wood bank robbery, open. Haven't been solved yet. The Atlanta Museum heist, open and I don't think it will ever get solved. The girlfriend of Kane, who I still believe murdered his teacher. She was kidnapped, raped, put in a coma, and almost blown to kingdom come. Open and hasn't been solved yet. Rick helped investigate all of those cases and I won't lie, he ran a very good and detailed profile on each one. That's one thing he does do better than any other officer I've ever worked with. I couldn't figure out the problem. He was out there doing what I need to be doing and they have me here doing what he needs to be doing. I felt like it's been long enough. I can get back out there and do what I do best. For the past seven years, I've worked all of the tough cases. Either by myself or with a team. I'm the man. Speaking of the devil, here he comes now with his curly blond hair and blue eyes. Just as I expected. I happened to look back and see him walking my way with two cups. This guy doesn't get it. I don't want your damn coffee, Rick. Trying to be nice to a rookie and got myself in some bullshit. If I would have known he was going to bring something that awful every single day. I would've turned him down from the start. I turned around to face my desk. Please don't let him come over here, please don't let him come over here. C'mon, God never answers my prayers. Rick popped in front of my desk like a good partner. Sure enough, he was about to offer me one of the cups. "Jordan, my man." He smiled. "Brought you the finest cup of fresh coffee in town." I pointed to my get the hell away from my desk, I got my own cup of coffee. "I'm good my friend. Thanks, but I already made some earlier this morning." His face frowned up and he kind of looked sad. "Oh, come on. A second cup wouldn't hurt? Drink with me?" He asked while sitting the steaming cup next to my own. "Second," I said with sarcasm. "I have been here since four in the morning my good man. I'm on my third cup. You're two cups behind. So, you keep it. You got some catching up to do." I lied. Hopefully, it worked. "Four in the morning?" He sighed. "That's a little early for you. I have to start getting out of bed sooner. Well, I guess I have two to get started." He looked at the paperwork on my desk. He took a sip of his dark, no sugar, nasty coffee. "Um, what you have going on?" "Trying to get ahead and finish this reluctant paperwork." "Oh, good. That means you get a chance to hit the field with me today. You know our kidnapped victim, right? Well, I have a lead on the other suspect. I'm following up today and that's not the good part. You want to check it out with me?" He asked. "Nah." I whispered. I have better things to do today than a lame follow up. Hell, that type of work wasn't exciting to me. Running around hoping that the bad guy will pop up. Boring. I'll leave that to him. "I feel kind of sick, too much coffee. When I finish here, I'll probably go on home and catch some sleep." "Oh, ok." He sounded unhappy. "Call me if you change your mind. It'll be exciting." I bet it will.

Chapter 27
READY FOR WHATEVER -KANE-

What I saw in the yearbook had a paralyzing effect on my mind. The pictures really fucked with my head. I have to get the hell out of here. My phone was blowing up. Smoke was sending text messages telling me to get the hell out of the house. Time was running out and I was standing there as if I wanted to get caught, staring at the pictures. I strapped the backpack around my shoulders. I grabbed it because I needed something to carry the books while I was on the move. It was the first thing in sight so someone will be mad about it missing. Their loss, they'll forgive me one day. It's only a bag. I ran to the front of the house and peeked out an upstairs window in the guest room. Shit, bad news. Abel pulled back in the driveway with his friends. Smoke wasn't parked in front of the house. He was smart enough not to be seen. I don't have time to figure out where he went. I was already pushing it. I don't want my brother and his nerd friends to catch me in the house. He'll ask all types of questions I don't want to answer. We haven't been quite on the same page as of late. Every time we tried to talk, I end up putting my hands on him. The last time that happened he told me, he'll be more than happy to send me back to jail. That's what you call a brother. I hurried back to my room at a top-flight speed. I lifted the window and climbed out. I held on the vine tree while I shut it. I got halfway down and without thinking about it, jumped. I landed on my feet and bent low to support the fall. Better than a cat would have done. I bolted through the backyard and hopped over a brick wall into the neighbor's yard. Dammit, I forgot they have an enormous bull mastiff, Coju looking attack dog that was ever created. And he was already en route. No room for bitching up or any second thoughts about climbing back over. I had one chance to make it out alive. I timed it perfectly, every step. His momentum would be his downfall. Patches of grass tore from the ground as he aggressively ran at me. His muscles weren't average for a dog. He didn't look like he wanted to play catch and that told me he was ready to bite a chunk of flesh out my ass. It was scary just thinking about how he wanted to do me. Five, four, three, two... He leaped into the air in attack mode. One, I grabbed the dog in midair while sidestepping his attack. I slammed his big ass headfirst into the brick wall behind me. I didn't stay to see the effect it had on him. I instantly shot out of a cannon to the front of the yard and hopped the wall to safety. I jogged to the sidewalk, panting as if I ran a mile. I reached down in my pocket and called Smoke while walking and trying to catch my breath. I was exhausted, too much had happened at once. I used to run like that with no problem back in school. Two years of sitting in jail got me out of shape. That was a good workout. Smoke answered and I told him where to pick me up. He pulled around in no time and I hopped in the car. "Damn, you cleaned up in there didn't you?" He asked, noticing the backpack. I took off the bag. "Man... you won't believe what I found," I said, rummaging through the bag for the yearbook. There was a laptop inside along with what I swiped. I pulled out the book and showed him the pictures of Alfred Ben, my brother, and the evil woman from the museum. He almost wrecked the vehicle when he saw the photo. This shit is crazy. All of them are friends and attend the same school. I found the name of the woman next to her picture, Gina. I wonder if Alfred, Gina, and my brother still get along, or is it just a coincidence. I put the yearbook back in the backpack and I grabbed the black notebook. My heart fell to the floor. Definitely my father's handwriting. I saw his penmanship too many times at the office. I can tell his handwriting from a mile away. I scanned the pages. There were all types of names of guns, locations, purchases, and shipment dates. On the next page, I found a list of countries and contacts. Prominent men and women, world leaders. The next few pages were people who owed or paid him money for the weapons. After turning the page, I read names on an order list with arrival times and shipment dates of different kinds of supply. The last page was bizarre. It was the name of my father's alias Bill Right and all of his foreign bank accounts. I counted an easy seven hundred million dollars. Damn, we didn't live like it. Maybe the money was safer in foreign accounts? It was close to a billion. Smoke kept asking what I was looking at, but the notebook held my attention. I didn't want to read anymore or believe it. The FBI agent was right. My phone started to ring. The only thing I could think about was my father being a gun smuggler. I finally answered the phone. It was The Planner. "Time to work."

Chapter 28
RETURNING GROUNDS

I got off the phone with The Planner. It's game time. I told him to meet me at the spot where his boy Ke'Mo Cut tried to kill me. That's a good place to do what I have planned. There's no one around and it's a discrete location. An abandoned warehouse with the right amount of cover just in case the situation got ugly. One hour until showtime. I wasn't going out like the last time. I'll protect my head for sure. I have a ton of stuff to worry about and put in perspective. The yearbook and the black notebook will have to wait. My main priority is The Planner and making sure I don't catch a bullet. I have to get focus. I put the notebook inside the backpack as we pulled into the apartments for a quick stop. Redd and Bear should arrive any minute. Smoke followed as I got out of the car. I opened the door and immediately went to the closet. I tossed the bag in the corner and grabbed my Beretta. I tucked it and went to the living room. I gave Smoke the diamond. He will hold on to it this time. He'll bring it in when I verify the money. It will only make me vulnerable if I have it on me. If The Planner knew the location of the diamond. I could kiss the money goodbye. I knew Smoke had his pistol on him, but I asked anyway. Better safe than sorry. Redd called my phone and I told them to come up. They came through the door and I asked them the same question I just asked Smoke. They were good, but I felt it wasn't good enough. The guns Smoke and I jacked from the kid were still in my closet in a black bag. I retrieved the bag and tossed it in the middle of the floor. Everyone grabbed a machine gun except me. I couldn't carry that much firepower because it would cause curiosity. I'm not planning an armed robbery. I'm prepared and have proper backup if necessary. I only want to get my money and get the hell out alive. We all left the apartment and loaded up in the vehicle. We went straight to the warehouse. On the way there, I thought about what kind of situation I'm about to get into with The Planner. I'm trying to avoid feeling tense. Is 2.5 million dollars, really worth my life? I thought about everyone I love and their situations. Smoke, Redd, and Bear were all going into this situation for 500 thousand. Did they think that amount of money is worth their lives? My mother is in a mental hospital. Kim is in a coma and I'm not sure if she will recover. Her doctor isn't telling me anything hopeful. Her situation is also affecting

Smoke. He already caught a body and his grandmother died. He probably feels like he has nothing to lose. Redd didn't fully recover from a broken leg that ended his basketball career. He lost his college scholarships and now has to settle for a nine to five. I'm sure that played a part in making his decision. Bear has a problem that I couldn't even begin to imagine. A sleeping disorder, that's enough for me so I know it's enough for him. My brother is another story that I'll address if I survive. Two-point five million dollars... yes, that's enough money to risk my life as of right now. We pulled into the warehouse. Fifteen minutes before The Planner arrives. My life is about to change or... possibly end. We parked in the back of the building. I broke the lock on the back door. We hurried inside, empty with a ton of cover. We unlocked the main garage and pulled down a chain to open it. Smoke and Bear went back to the car. They were in the second part of my plan. Redd yelled back at me from the garage. "They're here." He climbed up a long ladder to the top of the building to get a birds-eye view for my protection. Good idea. I stood in the middle of the warehouse by myself waiting for The Planner to emerge. This is it, time to get the show on the road. There's no turning back. A Hummer pulled in followed by a limousine and another Hummer. Damn, I didn't expect The Planner to show up like this, but he's rich and has four million in cash that's our money.

Chapter 29
BLOOD ON MY HANDS

The three vehicles parked in the order in which they had arrived. Man, it was starting to get intense. So many things were running in my mind that I couldn't remain focused. I didn't allow myself to panic. I still have the upper hand. The ace of spades rested in my hand. I'm sure he won't forget I have the diamond. I'm prepared for the unexpected. The vehicles sat there for a moment. I began to wonder if they drove in using a remote control. I kept my composure even though there wasn't any activity. Damn, I wonder what the hell was going on inside the limo. That's the vehicle I pinned The Planner to be waiting inside. The Hummers were probably goons protecting him. No harm here, it's just me. I smirked at that thought. C'mon, get the hell out so we can get this over with. This was beginning to seem like a standoff between myself and the vehicles. The sad part was if they popped out with guns,

I'm dead. I checked my watch. It was one o'clock in the afternoon. My instincts eased my hand behind my back on the tool. I held a firm grip on it ready to murder the first one to act stupid. There are two high stacked pallets next to me. If there's a shootout, they'll provide excellent cover. Here we go, the doors of the Hummers opened simultaneously. About seven to ten guys got out. Black men wearing rebel army fatigue clothes. They all handled military assault weapons. No question, my life is about to end. What's going on? The Planner sent an army at me this time? The soldiers gathered around each other and they paid attention to one man. He spoke in a foreign language that I couldn't understand. His deep accent sounded African. Not to mention they appeared to be African. The leader is extremely massive, looks powerful, and built like a brick house. He held his hand up and spent his index finger in a circular motion. The soldiers broke out from around him like a football huddle. This took me by surprise. What the hell were they doing? Suddenly, their leader walked up to me. "Kane?" He asked in a broken American accent. I didn't answer. I responded by nodding my head while never breaking eye contact. He slung his assault rifle around his shoulder and he began to search me. I allowed him to avoid getting into it with these guys. When he realizes I'm not carrying the diamond, I figure I'll get an opportunity to explain my offer. His men were running around searching every inch of the warehouse thoroughly. They were looking for any type of threat. I figured that part out. The man searching me pulled my cell phone from my pocket and found the gun in my back waist. Damn, I have nothing to protect myself. He held the weapon out and shouted in his foreign language. He removed the clip and emptied the bullets at my feet. They rolled around as they hit the ground one by one. He gave me my phone and gun without the clip. He smiled slowing two front gold teeth as he placed the clip in his waistband. He removed the rifle from his back and held it in my direction. I heard one of the soldiers yell from high above. Suddenly, gunfire erupted. I stepped back, surprised. I thought the leader fired his weapon ending my life. When I realized I was not dead and still breathing. I knew the gunfire came from somewhere else. The soldier yelled from above again. I looked up towards the direction I thought the fire came from. What the...? Two soldiers tossed something huge over the rail. It was too dark and high up to make what was coming at us fast. A body crashed down and brutally smacked the pavement. "No!" I yelled and started towards it. The leader butted me with the end of his assault rifle. I bent down and held my mouth in pain. I heard the soldiers calling out in their language. Redd! I forgot he was up in the rafters. I looked over at my dead friend. I got him killed. The worst feeling in the world started to take over my mind. He was lifeless. The fall crippled his body. His legs were bent far out of position. Blood ran from his mouth freely and that wasn't the worst part. His eyes were wide and bloodshot red. They seemed to be focused on me. Horrible. The soldiers rounded up and surrounded me with their guns drawn. My life was over. I'm ready to die as the leader shouted more orders I couldn't understand. Fuck it, I picked myself up. They held their guns on me as I gathered myself to a standing position. Suddenly, the limousine doors open. Two men emerged, my vision was kind of blurry from the shot I took to the face. I heard a strong accent come from a large man in a suit. He was even more massive than the rest of the men, including the big guy who butted me. The soldiers scrambled over to his side. The smaller of the two men stepped to me and I couldn't believe my eyes. "You."

Chapter 30
HISTORY OF FUN

The man in front of me took my breath away. My vision became clear again. What the hell is he doing here? This is extremely against the rules. Is he a part of all of this? We held eye contact not intimidated by the cold stare from each other. I spoke up, "Special Agent Jordan, right?" I spit blood towards the ground. I felt completely disrespected. He was the man who arrested and tried to have me convicted. He also questioned me about my father's murder. Now my friend is lying on the ground dead and he doesn't look concerned. I desperately want to slap that stupid look off his face. "Where is the diamond?" He said nonchalantly. What! He knew I had the diamond. How? If he does, why didn't he arrest me for the robbery? "Diamond?" I asked sarcastically. I wanted to see his reaction. "Don't bullshit with me Kid. I didn't come out here to fuck around with you." He opened his suit jacket and drew his weapon and aimed at my face. That's when I knew how serious this so-called FBI agent was about the diamond. He's willing to blow my brains out. "Where is my money?" He smirked. "Oh, the four million is here. First, I want to see the diamond?" At that moment, I knew I had been played by the law this entire time. This evil person standing in front of me, the mastermind I know for sure is... The Planner. "I don't get the voice box treatment? What, I'm not good enough for it in front of your friends?" He smiled and butted me with his gun. "This will be the last time I'll ask and that was it." He barked. The blow knocked me to the ground a second time. I held my mouth thinking today I might break the world record for gun butts to the face. I glanced over at my friend, Redd. Then, I muscled myself back up thinking of not letting his life end for nothing. "Listen, you can kill me if you like, but let me tell you something. You'll never be able to find the diamond. Show me my money. Then I'll make the call and you can have your diamond. My people are on standby waiting for me to give them the order. If I fail to do so, they already know what to do and I don't have to tell you what that is." The Planner or special agent dick head called back to the African man in the suit. "He wants to see the money." I focused on what was happening behind the sellout cop. I noticed the huge African man suit has several badges and stripes on both arm sleeves. Even his hat has a gold badge on it.

He resembled a high-ranking officer of some kind. He had to be in charge. He spoke to the soldier who gun-butt me the first time. He ran off to the Hummer that was parked in the front of the limo. He hopped in the bed of the truck and threw back the cover. He tossed a briefcase to another soldier who had followed him. He covered the bed and hopped out. He grabbed the briefcase from the soldier and walked over to the larger man. The leader gave him more orders. I caught the end of it, Yes General. That's the only part I could understand. I was dealing with not only a dirty FBI agent but the General of an army. Which all started from a phone call I wish I had missed. This situation is getting deeper every breath I take. The soldier followed The General's orders and begun to walk in our direction. My eyes were probably the biggest they have ever been in my entire life. The briefcase contained a large amount of one hundred dollar bills in neat stacks. The soldier closed the case before handing it to me and then raised his weapon. I heard an African accent come from the soldier. "Diamond?" "He won't hesitate to kill you." The Planner smiled. "The African army is well known for torturing their enemies. I'm sure at this point you want to please the General by handing over his diamond?" I slowly reached down into my pocket and grabbed my phone. Man, I was holding four million dollars in the other. The feeling made me want to get this over faster than I could. I text Smoke fast as I could like a white girl on a weekend ready to party. I told him to bring the diamond and leave the guns in the passenger seat. I also mention for them to leave their doors open for cover. I didn't want to text for too long. The General might think something was fishy. He could easily have one of his men take me out and not for lunch. My only concern is the safety of my friends. Redd was already dead. I had to protect them. That's why I still have a trick up my sleeve for The Planner and... The General.

Chapter 31
A DIRTY BUSINESS

Smoke and Bear pulled the car into the warehouse. They got out and did exactly what I instructed. They stood behind the car doors. I wanted them to keep their guns hidden down on the seats. If the soldiers spot their weapons they would immediately try to kill them. That's what I assume happened to Redd. The General's men are savage. No questions, just kill. Even though the weapons are hidden, they're in arm's reach. They both looked shocked when they noticed the African soldiers with AK-47 assault rifles. I told The Planner to walk with me to the middle to retrieve the diamond. He nodded and we began to walk over. Smoke began slowly moving forward and noticed Redd in a pool of blood. It was a tragedy. I picked up the pace because I didn't want his mind focusing on Redd. There's no telling what he'll do. We approached him. "Smoke," I said to get his attention off our dead friend. The African soldier pushed me in the back with his gun trying to speed up the process. "The Diamond, hand it over." The dirty agent held out his hand. Smoke looked at me and I signed that I have the money in the suitcase. He probably didn't notice it because his head wasn't all the way clear. He revealed the diamond and placed it in The Planner's filthy hands. The dirty agent holstered his gun and held the diamond up to the light, gawking at it. I glanced down at my watch. One minute. "Are we good?" "Change of plans. Now that I have the diamond, I can't let you leave. You might give away my identity. Grab him!" I knew this was coming. The Planner didn't want me to live through this transaction. The soldier grabbed me from behind. I shot my eyes at Smoke, he didn't move. We planned for this to happen. The Planner walked over to the General. I've been counting down from sixty seconds in my head. It's time. About twenty police cars swerved in taking The Planner and the African army by surprise. I'm more masculine than the soldier who held me captive. I know I can take him with ease. The army started firing at the police. I flipped the soldier over my shoulder and gave him a mean punch to the face. He immediately blacked out and I took his weapon. I heard bullets zipping past my head. I ducked and ran for cover. I used the pallets as a shield. I peered over to the officers. They were all shielded behind their vehicles. I noticed agent Rick returning fire at the African soldiers. I had called Rick the next night after

I finished planning with my crew. He gave me his number at the hospital. I told him that Ke'Mo was bragging about a black diamond and how he would be a rich man after the deal. After Ke'Mo took his own life, I let him know I found the diamond. His boss somehow found out and wanted my head for it. I also mentioned that The Planner wanted me to deliver it in exchange for my life. I didn't have to get detailed because Rick would have the biggest case solved of his career, the Black African Diamond. He was more than happy to agree. His job was to bring the police force and arrive precisely at 1:20 pm. That's when the deal would go down. So far, he didn't know I was involved in the diamond heist. Everything was going according to plan. I glanced at Smoke. He had safely made it to the vehicle. Smoke and Bear were firing at the Africans. From there, I moved to the other side of the pallet. The General had his gun aimed at The Planner. He was out-numbered by the Africans and reluctantly tossed over the diamond. The General along with three of the soldiers hopped in the second Hummer. The Planner drew his weapon and started firing at the vehicle. Damn, that's when I noticed the briefcase was in the middle of the commotion. I had dropped it when the Africans fired in my direction. Gunfire zipped back and forth between the police and the Africans. There was no way to get the case without taking a bullet. Shit, I have to take a chance. I ran out of cover sideways with the assault rifle doing what it does best. I grabbed the briefcase while firing with one hand and moving in the opposite direction. I took cover behind the limo. I crept to the front of the Hummer and opened the driver's side door, hoping the keys were still in the ignition. Suddenly, I got shot in the arm. Fuck! It stung like hell and I dropped the briefcase and grabbed the wound. I hopped in the vehicle fearing for my life. Luckily, I guessed right. I started the truck and made my escape from the warehouse.

Chapter 32
TEN MINUTES AGO -JORDAN-

I held my hand out. Kane's punk friend looked scared to give me the diamond as he should be. When I get the rock, they're dead. The kid looked over at Kane before finally revealing it. Yes, that's what I'm talking about. Give me the diamond you dirty rascal. He held his hand out and dropped it in my mine. I closed my hand immediately and drew back a bit to make sure nothing funny happened. I holstered my weapon. I held the diamond up to the light. It was dim in the warehouse. I needed a good look before handing it over to the General and his savage army from hell. I worked my ass off for it and I had to be the first to see its beauty outside of the case. Fifty million dollars here I come, baby. I heard the little dread head punk speak to me, "Are we good?" I'm good, but you're not. He held four million more dollars of my money. I want Kane dead. He made me look bad in front of millions of people. I was all over the news as the FBI agent who arrested a kid who beat one of the most advertised murder cases in the city. Not only did he make me look like a fool in the public eye. It was the only case I have ever lost in my star career. My revenge is set on him and his family. "Change of plans. Now that I have the diamond, I can't let you leave. You might give away my identity. Grab him!" I ordered the African soldier. I made my way over to victory to finish off the deal with the General. I saw the look on his face that he was pleased. I held the diamond up without giving it to him. "Here's the diamond I promised you. Where's my retirement?" "The bed of the front Hummer. Take the money and the vehicle where you please. Two large cases of money, 23 million stuffed in each one. Now give me the diamond." When I reached my hand out I heard police sirens. I swiftly turned around. Squad cars were pulling in to take care of me and the General's army. My career is over. That's unbelievable. How in the hell did the police know about the deal and the location? I'm sure as hell that I wasn't followed. I saw Kane flipped the guard over his shoulder and punch him in the face. Lightwork for a kid that big. That's when it hit me, Kane set me up. The police started to unload into the warehouse. I was caught by surprise. The General busted me in the back of the head with a pistol. I stumbled forward and turned around. His men were spreading out and began to open fire at anything moving. "You fool. You will die!" The General said sternly. There was nothing I could do. I was about to die. I held my hands up to make sure the General could see the diamond. I tossed it high in the air and watched his eyes as he went for it. I had a single chance to escape with the Africans occupied. I drew my weapon faster than a cowboy in the Wild Wild West. I exploded a slug in the guard nearest to me and then ran for cover. I ducked behind some pallets by the limo. I was breathing heavily as my heart raced from being too excited, game on pussies. My life was on the line. My adrenaline began to pump. I slid down to the opposite end while protecting myself. Shit! I couldn't believe who I saw. Rick! Out of all the fucking cops in the world. Kane set me up with my own fucking partner. I smiled, he's good. I slid back to the other end of the pallet. The General and three of his men got in the Hummer parked behind the limo. They backed out and I quickly revealed myself. I aimed at the front windshield trying to get a headshot on the General. The Hummer was well armored. They recklessly crashed their way through police cars. Fuck! They got away. It didn't matter. The Hummer with the two suitcases was my only concern. I looked to my left and heard assault fire closing in my direction. Kane! He was shooting at the Africans. I ducked back in cover and kept my attention on him. He grabbed the briefcase in mid-motion. My money! He hid behind the limo and crept towards the Hummer. He didn't notice me on the prowl. He opened the door of the vehicle and I fired my last bullet. Fuck, I had to reload. I saw him drop the briefcase and jump in the truck. Fuck, fuck, fuck! My retirement plan drove off. I ran towards the briefcase and grabbed it off the ground. I heard. Freeze, from behind. I turned around and saw Rick aiming his gun at me. "Seems like you're not a bad detective, after all, rookie." "Drop the weapon and the briefcase you piece of shit." Rick was trying to sound like me. I trained him well. I wasn't about to go to prison. I'll rot in there from the amount of time they'll give me. I threw the briefcase at Rick with all my might. I followed up with gunfire and took cover. I spotted a back door. I ran over without getting my head blown off. See you cop suckers later. I have a date with Mrs. Simmons.

Chapter 33
MOTHER KNOWS BEST -KANE-

I drove the Hummer with excruciating pain in my right arm. I made sure I was a safe distance before I pulled over. I needed to find a first aid kit or something to stop from bleeding to death. I don't want my arm to get infected. I searched the glove compartment and there wasn't anything useful. I hopped out while holding my arm and opened the back door. In some vehicles, you can find a kit under the back seat. I checked both sides, nothing. I tried to lift the seat and it wouldn't budge. I closed the door and made my way around to the back of the Hummer. I toss back the cover and hopped in the bed of the truck. I was completely taken by surprise by what I saw. Two very large aluminum suitcases that are ten times the size as the briefcase I had in the warehouse. Then, I remembered. The African soldier grabbed the briefcase I had from the bed of this truck. I bent down and unlocked one of the cases. Shit! There's a lot of money inside. I checked the second case and it's full of money. I sighed, taking it all in. Damn, I couldn't believe my eyes. I just became a millionaire. I smiled. That's the only thing I could do as I thought about the General. When the General finds out the diamond is a big fat ass fake cubic zirconia. He'll probably kill a few of his men and then The Planner. The day I went to the jewelry store to purchase Kim a diamond ring. I took the brochure I got from the museum the day I scoped it out with Kim. I showed him the diamond inside of it. I told him I like it and if he could make a replica. It cost no more than the rest of the money I had after buying the ring. Seven hundred, leaving me an extra three hundred. I gave him the entire thousand and he got started immediately. I still have the original diamond at home in the closet. I smiled again. Not only do I have even more money. I got the real diamond. I noticed a compartment and opened it. There was a gun inside a holster and a first aid kit. Lucky, me. I patched myself up the same way Kim did for Bear. That's when I thought about my boys. Damn, I hope they're safe. I covered the bed of the Hummer and hopped in the driver seat. I called Smoke and Bear cell phones. No answer. Shit! I pulled off, heading home. I got there in no time. I unloaded the suitcases into the apartment and took a long shower. When I got out, I heard a knock at the door. I looked through the peephole. My boys! I opened the door. We talked about everything that happened before I pulled out one of the suitcases. We counted the money all morning. Twenty-three million dollars! Damn, I gave Smoke and Bear ten million dollars apiece and the other three million will go to Redd's mother. That means I have at least 23 million in the other suitcase. I told them to lay low and they agreed. Rick had called me and I explained to him that I was alright. He said agent Jordan was a dirty cop and to watch my back because he got away. He offered protection. I thanked him, but I didn't need it. I told him to beef it up around Kim. Jordan might go after her. Rick told me he would do his best to bring him down. That was good enough for me. I trusted him. I drove the Hummer to the mental hospital. It's an all-black armored vehicle that belongs to no one. I was in a tank in case things got crazy. I parked the truck and walked into the building. I wasn't changing my daily routine because I have money. I want to appear broke until Kim came through. I'll move her and my mother far away after things cool down. Maybe we'll move to Jamaica. I signed in as usual and was led to the yard to meet my mother. What! Her progression was surprising. She wasn't sitting by the rose bush. I spotted her in a circle with other women. I walked over and pulled up a chair next to her. All of the women were smiling, even my mother. It made me feel better than ever. She looked at me and smiled. I wonder if she knows I'm her son? So, I told her. "I'm your son... Kane." She kept smiling at me. After a short moment, she turned back to the other women and said. "This is my son, Kane." My mother spoke! A lot of emotion ran through my body, but it turned from emotion to hate after what she said next. "I have another son, Abel. I don't claim him anymore because he murdered my husband."

Chapter 34
CHANGE OF PLANS

Abel sat in the living room in his parent's house with Gina, Bam, and Snake. They were coming up with a new plan. Ali's backpack was missing with Abel's laptop inside and that wasn't the only thing gone. His father's notebook was nowhere to be found. He tore the mansion apart searching for the book. The most important thing in his life is missing. The notebook was more valuable to him than the diamond. Making a deal with The Planner is out of the question after what he watched on the news. There was a shootout between the FBI and African soldiers. That had to be over the diamond. He thought about the Africans who originally owned the diamond and how Americans held it in a museum. The African army traveled to the United States after it was stolen by Kane. The Planner had to be involved. Over seven hundred million dollars was on the line. That's a crazy amount of money his father has in foreign bank accounts. There is no way he can get that money without the notebook. The diamond was supposed to give him a head start, but that plan failed. "We can go after the girl again?" Bam spoke up. "Security will be tight, but it's nothing we can't handle." "I don't think that will get the job done." Snake said. "The FBI is involved. After the African shootout with the police. I'm sure between the two, one of them has the diamond. Kidnapping the girl will be useless and risky." "What do you suggest?" Bam asked. "I think we should wait until the heat is down." Snake answered. "We will have to kill her, of course. She knows too much. Hopefully, she'll die in the coma so we won't have to do risk anyone being seen or captured." "That doesn't answer my question." Bam said with sarcasm. "What's the plan?" "Fuck the girl." Gina interrupted. "We need to find out who has the diamond." "How do you suppose we do that?" Bam shot his attention at Gina. "Sounds a little far-fetched." He crossed his arms and sighed as if he was waiting for the BS to spill from her lips. "Easy," She said. "We know where the girl lives. Kane is staying with her. We can break into the apartment and search for the diamond and most importantly, the notebook." She stood next to Abel. "That's a dumb idea." Bam retorted. "Kane doesn't have the diamond and he is too stupid to even care about the notebook." "Actually, Kane's intelligence doesn't play a part in having the notebook. Maybe he knew it belonged to his father. That's a good enough reason to take it along with Ali's bag. That doesn't mean he understands what's inside the book or on the laptop." Snake countered. "You need a password to unlock the computer so there is no way for Kane to search it." Abel lit a cigarette to calm his nerves. Gina's suggestion to break in Kim's apartment was a good idea. Kane is the only person who would want the notebook. Unless his father came back from the dead for it. He blew out a cloud of smoke and sighed. "Why would Kane want Ali's bag?" Bam said defensively. He felt like breaking into Kim's apartment would be a waste of time. What if Kane doesn't have the notebook or the diamond, then what? They'll be back at square one trying to figure out another plan. "We need the get the girl back." Abel was done listening to Bam nonsense. "No, Gina is right. We need to break into the apartment." Bam sighed. "Abel, that's..." "Quiet," Abel said sternly. "You're embarrassing yourself. You're smart enough to know Kim will be protected. She's in a coma, we don't have to worry about her speaking to the police. Like you said, what if my brother doesn't have the diamond? Kidnapping her would be a waste of time when we can just kill her when the heat dies down. We can wait." Gina smirked at Bam. She wanted to make sure he saw her devilish smile. Bam was pissed at Gina and Abel. He didn't like being made out to be a fool. Especially, by a girl whose brain isn't comparable to his own. Gina was more of a bitch to him than anyone else in the group. At first, he felt she was after Ali. Now he's gone and she's after him. Abel and Snake are best friends. She wouldn't bother Snake until after he's gone. I need to keep a close eye on this bitch, he thought. She's trying to ease her way to the top. Take us out one by one. She wants all the money for herself. Just what I expected, a money-hungry bitch who thinks she can outsmart me. I'll play your little game. He smiled back sarcastically. Abel continued. "My house was broken into and the only items missing are the notebook, Ali's backpack, and my laptop. Who do you think took it? The police, kids, thugs looking for my father? Nothing was broken and there is no sign of forced entry. I remember when I was a kid, Kane used to sneak out of the house through his room window. He left it unlocked. There's a tree outside it, he would climb down. I caught him a few times sneaking out at night. I made him pay to keep my mouth shut." He puffed on his cigarette. The room became quiet. He continued. "When I walked into his room this morning. I felt a slight breeze coming from the window. It was unlocked and not completely shut. At first, I thought nothing of it. It's always unlocked, but I don't remember it being opened. I changed the locks to the front and back doors of the house. Kane doesn't have a key. It's his only way in if he came home." Gina, Bam, and Snake were all in deep thought after what Abel said to them.

Bam was in his feelings after Abel didn't agree with him over Gina. His mind was clouded by his ultimate goal. Snake felt absolutely sure Kane was the person who stole the notebook. Killing Kim is important, but the laptop and the black notebook are at the top of the list. Gina felt more power each time Abel agreed with her. If only she could be his number one. Abel is her other half and no one will get in the way of her plans. No Bam, no Snake, no problem. "It's settled," Abel spoke up after observing everyone in the room. "Let's get to work."

Chapter 35
LOST AGENT -JORDAN-

For the past two weeks, I've hiding out in an abandoned mansion that belonged to the godfather of The Mafia Family aka TMF. The house was seized by the FBI when the don was taken into custody. Thanks to yours truly. The don received a life sentence and the house was never put back on the market. The FBI claimed ownership of the property, but I purposely misplaced some paperwork on the mansion and now it's unaccounted for, completely off the books. I thought, in case of an emergency the compound could be a good hideaway. That's better than turning it into an FBI headquarters or selling it to some rich guy who thinks he's the next Don Corleone. The only thing I thought about was murdering Kane Simmons for ruining my plans with the General. There is no way I'll ever get another buyer at fifty million dollars. The Africans are no longer working with me. The General will send his goons to murder me eventually. I lost my job. The diamond was long gone and Kane drove away in the Hummer with my money. If there's any type of shot at fixing this ugly situation. It will start by getting the money from Kane. After whiteboy Rick discovered I was involved with the Africans. Its gonna be hard to move as an FBI agent. Special Agent Jordan is on every department's big board in the state. I have to move fast and plan with caution. Since the shakedown at the warehouse, I've been waiting to make a move. The more time I lose, Kane will have a better opportunity to get away with my millions. I walked around the mansion with my hands behind my back as if I owned the place. Everything in the mansion looked expensive. Tall ceilings, marble floors, gold trim around the entire house, twelve gigantic bedrooms, five marvelous bathrooms, and a kitchen the size of a restaurant. I imagined owning the mansion and coming home every day to this place. But that's not reality. When I take back the money from Kane, I'll be able to purchase a mansion of my own. The first thing I'll do is get a new identity. The second thing, relocate somewhere off the grid where I can safely spend my new wealth without worrying about the FBI kicking in my front door. After two years of being undercover as a gangster in TMF. I know the right criminals that can make my dream a reality. I walked to the bar that was located below the house. I poured a drink and took a seat on one of the stools. I sighed after taking a sip. "Good stuff." I swirled the ice around in the glass thinking about what I got myself into for the past month. I didn't want to be a detective anyway. I kind of enjoy being a bad guy. It's more fun. When I worked with TMF as a mafia member my life was more exciting. I had money, cars, respect, and any woman I wanted. Although, that wasn't who I was in real life. The FBI created that person for me. I didn't worry about getting busted or going down for murder after I offed a guy. That's the life I want to live and Kane is preventing that from happening. I downed the drink and began to feel a bit saucy. Damn. I got up from the sit and swiftly grabbed the bottle of liquor by the neck while spinning in one motion. I drank straight from the bottle. I'm in this big ass house with nobody to talk to. I took another gulp. The Planner, baby. That's me, the bad guy. I stumbled over to the window. I normally don't get drunk. The curtains opened automatically with the push of a button. The view was beautiful. I could see the city far off in the distance. That's mines, I own everything and everyone in it. I took another gulp. Kane! I yelled at the top of my lungs. I can't believe I got outsmarted by a punk kid. I sucked my teeth and stood in front of the window with wobbly legs that barely held up my body. I grabbed a gun from my waistband and held it in front of my face, staring it down. You wanna play rough... Okay, we'll play rough. Scarface is the fucking ultimate bad guy. I pushed another button and the glass to the window slid open. I walked out to the yard. There was enough land to host an NFL football game. I held the weapon in one hand and the bottle of liquor in the other. I took a nice gulp and looked at the bottle. I'm drunk. I spoke to the bottle before tossing it high in the air. I aimed my weapon and fired several shots at it, missing every single one. The bottle hit a high point and started descending. Oh, shit. I stumbled out of the way just in time before it cracked my head open. The bottle shattered on the ground where I once stood. That was close. I looked at my weapon while thinking something was wrong with it. I turned it side to side observing it skeptically. I aimed at the broken bottle and fired. That's what I'm talking about. I blew over the barrow satisfied with the results of my aiming ability. I stumbled back inside the house thinking about kidnapping Mrs. Simmons later tonight.

Chapter 36
NEW INFO -KANE-

After I left my mom at the hospital and pushed the Hummer back to the apartment. My mind was racing all over the place. I don't know how to comprehend what my mother just said to me. I have another son, Abel. I don't claim him anymore because he murdered my husband. I know she's in a mental hospital, but this could be what drove her crazy? All I know is that I need to find out what's going on fast. I don't know what to think right now. I maneuvered in and out of traffic trying not to crash into anyone or anything. Hopefully, the police won't pull me over because I'm not watching out for them. I have one thing on my mind and that's finding out what is going with everyone in my life. The photos of my brother and his friends. What happened to Kim and the reason why my father was murdered. I need to know these things and there is a possibility the laptop could shed some light on the situation. After my mother said that my brother murdered my father. I'm thinking there could be some information on the laptop because it belongs to him. I wondered why he wasn't in school and why he's been acting evil. After all these years of being together, growing up in the same household, and looking out for one another. He could murder our father? Well, come to think of it. He's never really looked out for me. I've been the one looking out for him. I pulled into the apartment and parked the tank. I'm in a frantic state of mind right now. I turned off the motor and got out. I swiftly ran up to the apartment leaping step after step. I don't know why I'm in a rush to find out bad news. Although this could be the answer I'm looking for and all along my mother knew what happened to my father. I don't have a clear reason, but I believe what she said. I might just be crazy for thinking that way. I fumbled the keys around in my hand, my nerves were bad. Finally, I got the door open and rushed straight to the room. I went inside the closet and bent down to retrieve the bag. I swiftly unzipped it not knowing what I was going to find. I grabbed the laptop and tossed the bag on the ground. The answer was in my hands. I sat down trying to settle myself, breathe easy. Alright, here we go. I slowly opened the laptop and as expected, enter password. Abel is super smart and I know there is no chance in hell I'll ever know his passcode. Dammit, I need to find someone who can hack it so I can at least see what he's been up to. I reached in my pocket and grabbed my phone. I dialed my best friend's number. The phone rang a few times before he picked up. "Yo, Smoke. Where you at?" "Yo, what's good," He answered. "I'm up the street washing my car." "I have some crazy news. You won't believe what happened today. I'm at the apartment, can you come through?" I asked. "Alright," He said. "Give me ten minutes." "Cool," I said. "See you then." I hung up the phone and closed the laptop. I didn't try cracking the password. Something worse could happen like completely locking the computer. All I could do was wait. What if Abel is hiding something or if he was working with the kids in the yearbook photos? I felt my blood boiling. Now wasn't the time to lose control. I'm supposed to be living my dream. If it wasn't for Abel murdering his teacher, which ruined everything for me. Maybe I could've been somebody? Life isn't supposed to be this hard. Now look at me, I'm a monster. I never thought about robbing a bank or stealing a diamond when I was growing up. I wanted to be like my father and that's when it hit me, the notebook. My father was somebody who sold guns, a Lord of War. Now that I know what he really did for a living. Would I have still followed in his footsteps? The real question is would he have told me? I would've worked hard my entire life only to become a damn gun smuggler in the end? Did my brother find out and that's why he decided to murder him? There were too many unanswered questions I'll never get an answer for. The evil woman, Gina. The Alfred Ben guy who played a part in kidnapping Kim. They could be working for Abel. I set the laptop down on the bed. I got up to walk back inside the closet. I looked at the backpack and sighed while walking over to grab it. I pulled out the notebook and the yearbook and sat down on the bed. I opened the yearbook first and scanned through the pages looking at every photo of Alfred Ben, my brother, and Gina. I'm starting to believe this wasn't a coincidence. Gina was in one picture with Abel, smiling like she was just having a wonderful time with her boyfriend. She's smart and went to Yale with my brother, he's smart. She tried to kill me at the museum over the diamond. There was someone else with her who shot down from the vent. It could've been Alfred Ben, the other guy next to them in the photo or my brother. She knew about Kim and she didn't go inside the museum with us. How did she know of her? Not to mention she tried to finish off Kim in the hospital using a bomb. That's some evil shit. I can't forget about Alfred, who was actually in the accident with Kim. Now that I'm thinking about it. There were two other guys with my brother when I was outside of the house. Gina was the woman who was with them. There are three other guys in the photo with my brother. Alfred was one of them so that makes two. They're in this together. Yale isn't even fucking in Atlanta. Why are they here? School isn't out yet. Maybe I'm thinking too hard about it? The sound of my mother's voice repeated in my head, hurting my soul. I have another son, Abel. I don't claim him anymore because he murdered my husband.

Chapter 37

HI MRS. SIMMONS -JORDAN-

I woke up later that night feeling a little bit better. The don has an enormous bed and let me tell you, it's very comfortable. I sat up and checked the time, 9 pm. That's still enough time to visit a special lady. I got myself together and grabbed my weapon. Things could get wild and I'm the perfect cowboy for the job. I know Kane still has the money. He isn't stupid enough to spend it just yet. The FBI will be all over his ass. I shouldn't have to worry about it once I kidnap Mrs. Simmons. I'm sure that's a fair trade, he wouldn't mind accepting. It is his mother. His father is dead and he doesn't want to plant her next to him. Easy money, I love this shit. I've been hiding out long enough. Rick shouldn't suspect me to go after Mrs. Simmons. I should be in the clear. The people at the hospital will think I'm still an FBI agent when I flash my badge.

I'll just walk in there and tell them I'm extracting Mrs. Simmons and moving her to a new location. There you have it. Money in the Bank. I made my way down to the don's garage. The don had several vehicles to choose from. I need to keep a low profile. Something not too flashy. I scanned a row of cars, Ferrari, Lamborghini, Bugatti, Benz, limousine, Corvette, BMW. Oh, here we go. A smooth Cadillac, baby. I found the keys to the Cadillac. It was a beautiful all-black old school model. Very nice and not noticeable. I started the vehicle. Damn, this bad boy sounds great. I left the garage on a mission. I put the pedal to the metal as I made my way through the city. I even turned on a Jazz radio station. It's the best music ever created. Ok, I'm lying. I love listening to heavy metal when I'm chasing down a bad guy. It's something about the sound that pumps me up when I'm ready to kick some ass. That reminds me of something. After I get my money from Kane. I'll kill Rick. I feel like he deserves to die after everything I did for him. It's only fair. I arrived at Hill Heights in under 30 minutes. The parking barely had any other vehicles. Only five cars were parked outside, plus my new Cadillac. I pulled up to the entrance. I need to leave as soon as possible after I nab her. I got my weapon ready. I switched the safety off just in case one of these crazy fuckers try to be a hero. I got out of the car and made my way into the building. Keep calm, this is your first time here. You're a cop, nobody should question your authority. I have a badge and a gun. That should be good enough. My face was on the news, tagged as a rogue cop. Who watches the news anyway? Oh yeah, people without a life. I got to the front desk. A lady was sitting there with her head down looking at her phone. She didn't notice me standing there. "Excuse me." I tried not to sound mean or cause any commotion. She didn't answer and began cracking up at whatever had her attention. "Excuse me." Nothing. I noticed a bell on the counter and I dinged it. Nothing. "Excuse me, I need help?" Nothing. Ok, ding, ding, ding... I went crazy on that fucking bell. How do you like me now, bitch? I wanted to blow off her head. She snatched the bell and placed it behind the desk without even raising her head. She pointed to a pen and pad. It was a sign-in sheet. What? I don't have time for a damn sign-in sheet. I'm the only person here, the sheet was empty. Suddenly, the TV in the lobby displayed the news alert. Shit, a picture of my face appeared on the screen. I reached for my gun. Her eyes were on the TV screen. I'll have to kill her right now. My finger was the trigger ready to end her life. Surprisingly, she looked back down at her phone and started laughing. She never looked at my face. I holstered my gun. "You better hurry up." She said. "Visiting hours are about to be over." Thankfully, I didn't have to drop her ghetto ass. I looked at the clock on the wall, 9:45. Visiting hours ended at ten. Damn, fifteen minutes. Think. I placed my badge in front of her face. "FBI, I need to know what room Mrs. Simmons is in?" She looked at the badge before she put her head back down. "Down the hall, second right, next left, third room on the right." She started laughing again. "I love George Jefferson. That man is a damn fool." She said while laughing. I put my badge away while shaking my head. "He isn't that damn funny," I said as I turned away. I heard her say, "Whateva." I walk towards Mrs. Simmons' room. I noticed a security guard at a snack machine. Dammit, he looked up as I walked passed. Fuck, I felt him walking behind me. "Aye," He called out. "You have ten minutes." I didn't turn around. "Gotcha," I called back. He might be a problem. I sped up. I wanted to check if he was still following me. "What room are you looking for?" C'mon, man. You don't want to die today. I reached for my gun unnoticed. I used my other hand to get the silencer I hid inside my jacket pocket. I kept walking as I screwed it on. "I said, what room are you looking for?" He pressed. He sounded closer. Five, four, three, two, one. I felt his hand grab onto my shoulder. I swiftly turned around and put three in his stomach. I caught him before he hit the ground. Night, night. I dragged him to a nearby closet and stuffed him inside. I read his nametag before I closed the door. That was your fault, Edward. I got to Mrs. Simmons' room and opened the door. "Hello," she was sound asleep in bed. I walked over and tapped her on the forehead. I smiled, but effective. Her eyes popped open. She looked shocked. When her vision became clear I flashed my badge. "Hi, Mrs. Simmons. I'm agent Jordan, but you can call me, The Planner."

Chapter 38
NEW FAMILY -KANE-

I heard a knock at the door. Smoke. I closed the yearbook and walked into the living room. I greeted my friend. "Smoke, thanks for sliding through." We dapped. "No problem." He walked in. "What's up? You sounded worried about something on the phone. Is everything straight?" I shut the door behind him. I looked him dead in the eyes and spoke seriously. "Hell no, some heavy shit got dropped on me that I need you to help me figure out." "Is it about what happened at the warehouse? I didn't spend any of the money." He looked worried. I walked past him. "Nah, we're good on that. It's something else." I saw a sign of relief on his face. "You might want to sit down for this one." I walked into the bedroom. "It's like that?" I heard him speak up from the living room. I walked back out with the backpack. "I think so." I took a seat and sat the bag next to me. For some reason, I felt my nerves acting up and needed to calm down. "Did you bring some Kush?" I'm not a smoker, but I need a hit. "Don't tell me all you want is some weed?" Smoke pulled out a sack. "You know I got you. I'm Smoke Dawg." He started breaking down weed on the table. The smell was super strong. "It'll be better if we smoke while I tell you about Abel. Trust me, this shit is crazy." He rolled the weed with rolling papers. "That serious, huh?" He fired up the blunt and took a puff. "Yeah," He passed it to me. I took a hit and surprisingly, I didn't choke. The taste was good. I could feel smoke entering my lungs and took another hit before passing it back. "Good stuff," I said while holding the smoke in my system. Damn, I felt high already. I sat back and thought about where I wanted to start. "Only the best." He blew a ring of smoke into the air. "What's up with your brother? Is he still pressing about the museum? I see you brought out the bag from the other day. He's hiding some shit with his sneaky ass?" He passed the blunt. I inhaled enough smoke to drop an elephant. It was a good minute before I slowly exhaled. I'm straight for sure and passed the blunt to Smoke. "I'm good." I sat up. "I think my brother figured out our dad was dealing weapons and murdered him." Smoke started choking uncontrollably and pounded on his chest a few times with his fist. "What the fuck." He coughed out. "Damn, my bad. I didn't expect that." He ash the blunt. Smoke eyes are low and fire red. That's what you call a super high. After he regained control of his lungs, I elaborated. "I'm going to make this as clear as possible. First, he murdered his teacher and let me take the blame. Second, he didn't show any emotion after the death of our father. Third, he called me after the museum heist and questioned my whereabouts. The girl from the museum tried to murder Kim. How does she know Kim and I are together? Her name is Gina by the way. She goes to school with my brother." I grabbed the yearbook from the bag and flipped to a page with her and Abel. I gave it to Smoke. "That's her, my brother and Alfred Ben. He's the guy who was in the van with Kim during the accident after she was kidnapped. He also went to school with my brother. I thought the two guys with them looked familiar when I saw the picture. They were with Abel when he left the house. I'm guessing The Planner called Abel about the diamond. Trying to play us against each other for the money. Gina wasn't alone at the museum. The black notebook was sitting out in the open. I'm sure that's what my brother was after. Everything from gun models, prices, contacts, and profit is in that notebook. My father wouldn't have something like this sitting around for someone to find. It'll be locked in a safe where no one could find it. Like, in his office hidden behind a wall in a closet." I paused and looked at Smoke. He was paying close attention to what I was saying. "I'm nowhere near smarter than my brother, but I'm not dumb. He got this from my father's office. My mother spoke today. She told a group of women about not claiming Abel because she thinks he murdered our father." I saw Smoke's mouth drop. "Damn, this is some serious shit." He flipped the page in the yearbook. "Your brother is in a few pictures with these people. You're right, they're working together. I think you're also right about The Planner putting him on the diamond. He's the agent who worked your case and your father's. He knows enough information about your family. He set up both of you. Abel needed help so he called for backup as you did with us. I wanted to tell you that the agent murdered your father after we discovered he was The Planner. Although, what your mom said and the notebook. I have to agree that your brother killed your pops. So, how do we go about handling this situation?" I grabbed the laptop from the bag. "There's a password entry on this laptop. It belongs to Abel. There could be some information on here that can help. One thing I know about my brother is that he researches and keep notes on everything he does. If there is a connection between everything I mentioned. It'll be on here. I just need to find someone smart enough to crack it. You know anybody with that skill set?" "I know someone." Smoke reached in his pocket and pulled out his cell phone. "You remember Jimmy Tang?" "The Asian kid we went to school with?" "Yeah, he works for a big tech company." Smoke scrolled through his phone. "I ran into him the other day at the gas station. Good thing we stopped those kids from giving him a swirly. He still wants to be down with us." "I think it's time to add him to the crew." I grabbed the blunt from the ashtray and sparked it. I blew out smoke feeling my body relax again. I'm glad Smoke is helping instead of thinking I'm crazy. Smoke put the phone to his ear. "Yo, Tang. You still wanna be down with the crew?"

Chapter 39
TWO BABIES

Abel checked his watch. His mind was made up after carefully planning their next move. Getting the notebook back is critical. He thought about killing Kane if he does have the black book. What good will come of it if that is his final decision? Nothing, Kane is worth nothing. He doesn't consider him as a brother. Kane is just another knucklehead who happened to enter this world at the same time as him. There is a certain level of intelligence you have to possess for Abel to even consider you as a friend. Yet alone, a brother. Gina, Bam, and Snake surrounded him, patiently waiting for their orders. Gina couldn't wait to prove herself. Snake is on Abel's side no matter what, even if he wanted him to kill Kane, that wouldn't be a problem. On the inside, Snake wished he was Abel's brother instead of Kane. Bam's stare could have pierced Gina's soul. He thought something was fishy with her and made it a goal to find out. Hopefully, Abel's plan included him without her. Whatever it takes to keep her on the other side of the fence, he'll welcome. "This is what I need to be done." Abel looked at each of them. His plan didn't take long to form. Simple, nothing complicated. "Snake, I want you to take the lead on this one. You already know the apartment where Kane is staying. After you're sure he isn't there, get my notebook. Before you break-in, check the top lining of the door or the floor mat. Kane's old fashioned. There's a possibility he stashed a spare key close by." He watched Snake nod. "Don't trash the place. I want you to be unobtrusive. The longer it takes for him to figure out what happened, the better. Bam, I want you to go be his lookout. That's all I need you to do, simple. This isn't a museum heist. We're talking about a dumb kid who isn't smarter than a grapefruit. This shouldn't be difficult." Gina's face turned up. "What do you want me to do?" "Cook," Bam suggested. He had a smirk on his face. Snake, let out a light chuckle. Gina got in Bam's face with closed fists, but Abel stopped her in time. She was furious. "Stop," Abel held her arm. Gina was stronger than he thought. She nearly pulled away. "You two need to work out your differences if you want us to be successful. There is a lot of money on the line. Stop acting like two babies." Gina reluctantly resisted the urge to knock Bam lights out. She'll never forget what he said until it's handled. Once she has her sights on unfinished business. She destroys the problem. Bam met her stare, I have you where I want you. He wished she could read his mind. He wanted her to know that he'll kill her if it came down to it. Nothing will prevent him from getting his share and being on Abel's good side. Abel is the smartest person he ever met and his only true friend that views the world through the same microscope. "I apologize for what I said." He didn't sound apologetic. He saw the look in Gina's eyes and could have sworn they turned an evil red before she walked away. Gina didn't buy Bam's bullshit apology. She wanted to finish him right then for disrespecting her as a woman. That's one thing she doesn't tolerate. She walked away before things got worse. She went upstairs to Abel's bedroom and slammed the door. She was furious about not being a part of the plan. She wanted to prove herself to him. She wants to be his number one and getting there doesn't include not being a part of the plan. Abel sighed. He doesn't like it when she's pissed. There's no telling what she'll do. Her actions are unpredictable. I'll take care of her later, he thought. He turned his attention back to Snake and Bam. "You two know what to do. The notebook is our main goal. I know he has the book. I can feel it. Don't let anything else distract you. This is the most important thing in my life and yours. If we can't get through this simple task, how will we ever corrupt the government? Kane doesn't know the power the notebook holds.

I need that book in my hands tonight. Now go." Snake and Bam left the mansion on the move. Snake drove to Kim's apartment. He parked in a discreet location, thinking Kane doesn't have any knowledge of who they are but rather remain at a safe distance. He wanted to make sure the coast is clear before making a move. Abel clearly stated he didn't want any fuck ups. This job is more important than their lives. Their only goal is to find the black notebook. Bam adjusted his seat. He was beginning to feel uncomfortable. "How long do we have to wait?" They have been waiting outside the apartment building for two hours. Snake remained silent and focused all of his attention on the apartment. Bam began to get frustrated. The car was off and the heat from the sun was furious. The temperature was well over ninety degrees in the car. "Let's move, nobody's home. This is our opportunity." He popped the lock on the door. Snake quickly pressed the lock button, securing all doors. "Are you stupid?" He pointed to Kim's car. "That's the girl's car parked next to the Hummer. He's here, be patient or explain to Mind Bandit how you fucked up the plan." Bam stared at the car dumbfounded. How could he be so stupid and blind to the fact that the car belonged to the girl they had kidnapped. He didn't see it because the Hummer was blocking his view. It nearly cost them the mission. He began to think about what would Abel think of him if that had happened? If he would still consider him a friend? Abel is the only person who recognized his true potential. I can't mess this up, he thought. I have to be on point. Gina played a part by throwing off his focus because his mind was wrapped around her true intentions. He couldn't bring the information to Abel without proper evidence. He exhaled and waited for Snake's order. Be a lookout, that was his job. Even when Snake goes inside the apartment, he'll have to wait in the car regardless. "There," Snake watched Kane and another man leave the apartment. "Easy peasy." Bam sank in his seat, feeling like the dumbest person on earth while watching them walk down the steps. If Gina was here, she would've given him a mouth full. Luckily, she was ordered to stay at the house. I hope he doesn't tell Mind Bandit about this. He wanted to avoid any embarrassment. "They're leaving, let me be very clear on something. Don't try anything out of the ordinary. I don't want to get caught behind your idiocy. All you need to do is look out for me. Nothing more, nothing less, understand?" Snake didn't look in his direction. He kept his attention on Kane. Bam hated being treated like a baby. Who does he think I am, calling me an idiot? I'm the smartest person besides Mind bandit he's ever met. Bam wanted to say something, but he held his tongue. When all is well and done, he'll show Snake who's the idiot. "No problem," He saw the brake lights on the vehicle. "I'll call if they return. Remember, don't destroy the apartment." At this point, he wanted to sound like he clearly understood Abel's orders. Snake gave him an unimpressed look. Snake smirked. Bam was trying to keep his ass from being grass. He wasn't planning on mentioning Bam's stupidity. His only concern was the notebook and not getting caught. Snitching on Bam wasn't worth the trouble it would bring. His intelligence isn't that low for something he thought was a completely irrelevant comment. Snake noticed they drove in another vehicle and not the girl's car. The vehicle backed out from the parking space and left the neighborhood. He waited five extra minutes before deciding to make a move. "Ok, I'm going inside so watch my back." Bam nodded and he exited the vehicle. He looked both ways before he approached the building, trying not to appear suspicious wasn't that hard. It's not a bad neighborhood which made it easier for him to blend in. Thankfully, the apartment wasn't in the hood. Nobody around, he thought. He swiftly went up the stairs and put his ear to the door, listening for any sounds of activity. Everything seemed normal and it was quiet inside. He knocked on the door for insurance. Nobody's home. Abel said check the door lining and under the welcome mat for a spare key. He looked at his feet. There wasn't a mat. Ok, that cancels one hiding spot. He ran his hands on the top lining of the door. No key. One thing left to do, he thought. He reached in his pocket. "I guess I'll have to do this the hard way."

Chapter 40
JIMMY TANG -KANE-

I sat the bag next to the couch. All I need to take is the laptop. If there is something on this that points to my brother, I don't know what I'll do to him. My father meant a lot to me and I loved him with all of my heart. I don't care if he did live a secret life. He did it for his family, to create a better life for us in America. I know my father, he's a good man. I grabbed the keys to the apartment. I'm high as hell and the only good thing about it is Smoke's driving. I put on some dark shades before we left out. I wasn't comfortable with people seeing me in this state. It took us about twenty minutes to make it to Jimmy Tang's tech company. The place looked amazing from the outside. Tang Technologies, I read the sign displayed on the building. "It's a family business." Smoke said while turning off the car "Apparently, everybody in Tang's family is smart." He opened his door and got out. I stepped out of the car with the laptop.

"Most Asians are." I shut the door and looked at Smoke over the hood of the car. "Nah," he had a skeptical look on his face. "Most of them are dumb as hell. Don't play into that stereotype. They're just good at recognizing the few who are intelligent." He walked around the car. I shrugged my shoulders. Smoke might have been hanging around a few Asians while I was incarcerated. We walked through the front door. The inside of the building is enormous. Just looking around the place is something to behold. You wanna talk about technology? This place is loaded. I noticed a robot dog and for a second, I thought it was real. There were all kinds of futuristic-looking gadgets. I'm in nerd heaven. "This place is crazy," I muttered. "Yeah, they have some stuff in here that will make you think we're living in year 3000." He stopped. "Like this," he pointed at a woman. "Check her out." "C'mon, you know I'm with Kim." The woman is fine, but I would never cheat on my woman and he knew that for a fact. Maybe he was testing me? The woman walked over to us. "You're tripping," Smoke started laughing. "My guy, she's a Robot Babe created for nerds with no game. Don't trip. I thought she was a real person the first time I saw her." The robot spoke. "How are you doing today, honey?" She smiled. What the fuck? Am I that high? I'm not that high, am I? No way. Ok, Robot Babe sounded real, looks real, and I'll be damned if she's not equipped with huge breast. Not to mention, they had the nerve to dress her in a sexy maid uniform. I didn't know how to respond to Smoke or Robot Babe. "Hey babe." Smoke said. "I'm feeling horny. You want to get it on?" He slapped my shoulder with a big grin on his face. "Yes, honey." She responded. "How do you want it? I like it from the back." Robot Babe bent over and lifted up her skirt. "Come on, give it to me daddy." What! I can't believe what I'm seeing from this machine. They actually have products like this for sale? Unbelievable. I saw something that completely took my breath away. Robot Babe has an opening. And you know what I mean. "You can have sex with her? Are you serious?" "Hell, yeah. It'll cost you a cool fifty grand for that ass." He informed me. "Fifty thousand damn dollars." I began to feel embarrassed and uncomfortable. Robot Babe is bent over in front of me, not Smoke. Every eye in the building was on me like they were waiting for a show. Luckily, I have on dark shades. You couldn't pay me to nail this thing in front of all these people. Before I had a chance to react, Smoke did something wild. "Bang!" Smoke grabbed Robot Babe by the hips from behind and pretended to have sex with her. "Bang, bang, bang…" Everyone in the building began to laugh at my best friend. I slowly shook my head unable to defend myself. We're the only black guys in the building. Of course, we walked in together. Suddenly, I heard a familiar voice. "What I tell you about fucking my hoe, dawg?" An Asian dude in street clothes spoke. "I forgot to tell you she can get pregnant."

"Oh, shit." Smoke backed off. "Really?" I spoke up. "Hell no, fool." Jimmy Tang started cracking up. "We haven't figured out how to get these bitches pregnant, yet." "You're wild, my guy." Smoke dapped up Tang. "Kane you know Jimmy. This mofo is crazy and he acts black." "You know it." Tang held his fist out to me. "Pound that shit up." Tang still had an Asian accent while trying to sound black. I stared at the goofy look on his face. I have to say this kid is one of a kind. I gave him some pound. "Sup." Tang looked at what I was holding. "What's the laptop for? That shit broke or something?" "Actually," Smoke took over. "We wanted to know if you could crack the passcode." "What to fuck are you loud for?" The look on Tang's face was spontaneous. "Robot Babe, get the fuck out of here. You don't need to hear this shit." What? Now I'm lost. Jimmy's acting like the FBI was listening. "You good?" "You two fuckers want me to do some gangsta shit." Tang grabbed us by the shoulders and pushed us toward a back door. "Anybody could be listening." I looked around and personally, I don't think nobody gives a fuck. They appeared to be minding their business. We got to the back door. A weird looking keypad provided entry. Jimmy spoke to the keypad. "Jimmy Tang has a big dick." The lock clicked. "That's a unique passcode." I said while walking through the door. "Yeah, I know." Tang looked back and smiled. "It's easy to remember." "You know your dick isn't big." Smoke laughed.

"Bullshit," Tang countered. "You wanna see that shit?" He reached for his belt. "No!" Smoke and I spoke simultaneously. Damn, that was close. I definitely don't want to see his dick. He stopped and smiled. "You bitches know Asians have small dicks." Tang laughed. "That's why it's a good passcode." He led the way to the back. We walked down a long hallway. Finally, we reach another room with a keypad. Let me guess, this has something to do with his nuts? "Fried chicken and rice." Tang said. Ok, he got me. We walk into an enormous space with nothing in it but a table. It resembled an interrogation room, but larger. This brought back a few memories. "You have tight security for a room with nothing in it." "Only to the untrained eye." Tang said with a smile. "Watch this shit." I saw Tang place his right hand on the center of the table. A light illuminated around it. Suddenly, the ceiling lit up and a huge face of a woman appeared. I slowly turned to Smoke without taking my eyes off the face. "Tell me I'm not tripping?" "Crazy," I guess that was all Smoke could muster out. "You mean fucking insane," Tang said laughing. "This bitch took forty years to build." "Is that Salma Hayek?" Smoke spoke up. "You know it," Tang said coolly. "You know she's fifty-something," I said. "That's Dusk Till Dawn Salma Hayek." Tang blew her a kiss. "Whichever, I'll crush both." Smoke said. I shook my head. Something wasn't adding up. "You said this took forty years to build? You're like what, nineteen?" "That's funny," Tang said. My father started this project forty years ago. I recently began working on her for the past five years. And I'm sixteen by the way." "Damn, this entire time I thought you were our age." Smoke said highly. "Young ass." "That's what happens when you skip a few grades." Tang said. "Listen, I'm not here to talk about your age or play with your computer girlfriends." I told him. "Can you crack this or not?" "Give me that shit with your dumb a..." Tang stopped and looked me up and down. "Just hand me the laptop please." I gave him the computer. My size stopped him from saying something foolish that would've gotten his nose pushed in. Plus, I had a serious look on my face. Tang sat the laptop on the desk and turned it on. He looked up to the ceiling. "Salma baby, crack this motherfucker." I couldn't believe my eyes. A beam hit the computer like a ray of light from the bottom of a space ship. No way this is happening right now. I questioned myself rather or not I was dreaming. You don't see stuff like this on an everyday basis. Now I'm beginning to wonder what type of technology the government has in their possession. A few moments later, letters began to appear on the ceiling. The first letter was D, then I and E. DIE? After ten more seconds a K appeared, then A, N, E. I looked at Smoke and he didn't look high anymore. My brother's passcode is DIE KANE. Smoke looked me dead in the eyes. "He definitely murdered your father."

Chapter 41
CHECKPOINT

Snake reached in his pocket and grabbed a small device. There wasn't a way to get inside the apartment without causing some damage. Abel's brother didn't leave a key under the doormat or the lining of the door. No problem, he thought. He brought the small device to eye level. Time to put in some work little buddy. He placed the small mechanical spider on the ground. It was part of a science fair project at school. Snake took pride in the mechanical design because it was his best invention. Snake operated the spider from his cell phone. A tiny green light clicked on its back showing that the device had power. His phone displayed two knobs and a camera view to show what the spider was viewing. He moved his finger across the left knob and it took off under the door. Snake smiled. Moving the tiny spider was like playing a video game on his phone. He made it jump on the side of the door. He had a full view of the doorknob. He moved the device in that direction. It was faster than he thought. He looked away from the phone, checking if anyone was around watching him. The coast was clear. If there had been a problem, he wasn't doing anything wrong, but looking at his phone. He got back to work and pressed the tools tab. A drop-down menu appeared. He used the web option. He watched the spider shoot a string of webbing to the center of the knob. The thin string was made to be extremely strong. He made sure of that during creation. He made the spider move counterclockwise around the outside of the knob. One end of the web attached to its back and the other held the turn lock. After three circles, the lock clicked. Snake held a huge grin on his face. Spiderman my ass. Snake gripped the doorknob and turned. The door opened willingly. He walked through. He put the spider in his pocket after turning off the power. He looked around the apartment. Everything was nice and neat. This shouldn't be hard, he thought. He smelt a very strong scent of ganja. He never smoked pot before but could tell the difference between some good and bad weed. Whatever they smoked had to be powerful. He was getting lightheaded from secondhand smoke and he just walked through the door. They had to be fucked up, he thought. He scanned the living room. He didn't want to touch anything unless he had to. No way, he spotted a bag similar to Ali's. He walked over and picked it up. The name on the backpack read Ali's name. Yep, those guys were toasted. It was like they left it there for him. He opened the bag and found the yearbook and the black notebook. Yes. Abel will be proud of a job well done. Time to move. He zipped the backpack close and turned for the door. He felt the smell growing stronger under his nose. He paused, smoke was streaming from the table. He looked down and saw a nice rolled blunt in the ashtray. Funny, he didn't notice it when he walked in. It became tempting not to take a puff. Everyone at school talked about getting high. It's what cool kids do. At least at his school. Being smart isn't everything. He wanted to feel cool for once in his life. The thought of Abel entered his mind, telling him not to fuck this up. He placed the bag on the floor and sat down. The longer he procrastinated the higher he got. Why does Abel get to make all of the decisions? He took a deep breath and exhaled. It's already rolled and lit. He doesn't know anyone who sells weed. This will possibly be the only opportunity to smoke some. Fuck. He came to a decision. He reached for the blunt and grabbed it from the ashtray. Hell, he felt cool already. He put the blunt to his lips. Smoke hit his lungs before having a chance to take a single puff. He began to cough like an amateur for the first time. This is for every time I was left outside the party. He pulled on the blunt and the tip lit like Christmas while burning slowly. He held in the smoke. This isn't that bad, he thought. Suddenly, the smoke took control causing him to cough multiple times like he was dying. He pounded his chest to regain control over his body. Damn. He felt a little more relaxed than before. Am I high, he questioned? If I am, it's not enough. He giggled. He took another long drag. This time he did much better at maintaining self-control over the smoke. The smoke left his lungs into the air. He didn't feel normal anymore, he felt cool. He placed the blunt back in the ashtray. He hit his limit and knew it. Another hit would have finished him. Focus, he told himself. I have to get out of here. He got up and headed for the door. He put his hand on the knob and froze. Damn, I'm forgetting something. He turned around. His mind was blown. What the fuck did I come here to get? He contemplated for a moment. I can't be this high? He walked back over to the couch and sat down. Ok, I came through that door, why? I walked over here looking for something, what? He started giggling. I can't believe I forgot what I came here for. Abel is gonna be pissed when I tell him I forgot about the laptop and notebook. A great idea popped in his head. He clicked on a name in his cell phone. "Why are you calling me?" Bam spoke hectically. "Is everything clear out there?" Snake said, trying to bait him. "Yes, did you find the laptop and notebook?" Bam asked. "I sure did." Snake got the answer he wanted. He hung up the phone and grabbed the backpack. He stopped and looked down at the blunt. "Nah."

Chapter 42
BAD GUYS RULE -JORDAN-

I sped back to the mansion. I put Mrs. Simmons in the passenger seat and hate I did. This woman stared at the side of my face for the entire time without saying a word. What the fuck is her problem? I'm curious if she remembers that I was one of the officers at her husband's office? She was in shock after witnessing her husband shot dead on the floor. I wish I could replay that moment her face turned up, funny. Jar was just another Indian gunned down by a cowboy. I wonder if I slap that stupid look off her face, would she respond? I parked the Caddy in the garage. I looked at Mrs. Simmons. "Have you ever seen me before?" I need to know if this woman can identify me. She's good as dead after I get my money from her son. At this point, it doesn't matter if she knows my identity. She kept that same stupid look on her face. It's like I'm speaking to a dummy. At least I won't have to hear her mouth all night. Hell, she's unaware I kidnapped her. I got out of the car and walked around to the passenger's side. "C'mon, bitch." I know, I'm an evil sonofvabitch. At least I opened the door and helped her out of the vehicle. I'm just getting the hang of being a full-time bad guy. I walked her into the mansion. She didn't give me any problems when I got her out of the car. So far, so good. Let's keep it that way. She probably thinks this is a vacation resort compared to that nasty place she was staying in. Look at that, I did her a favor by getting her away from Hill Heights. "I don't know if you can understand me." I turned to her after shutting the door to the house. We stood in the hallway. "I had to remove you from Hill Heights. That place isn't safe for you anymore. You are much safer here with me. I have a room for you upstairs." I walked her down the hall as I spoke. She marveled at everything along the way from the paintings on the wall to the luxurious furniture sitting around the house. "I'm gonna call your son, Kane. And inform him of your whereabouts." Mrs. Simmons stopped and smiled at me. I showed her a fake smile. She won't be smiling after I put a bullet in his head. I'll kill him first just to see her stupid smile turn into a beautiful frown. We walked upstairs slowly, almost as if she was an old woman. Her husband's death left her fucked. I'm mean, she's around my age with a phenomenal body. She can have any man she wants. I've worked plenty of murder cases involving husbands and wives. And let me tell you, they move on after about three months. Rich women can't stand to be alone. We made it to the room and I opened the door for her. She was suspicious about entering the for a moment. I helped her out by giving her a little nudge on the back moving her past the threshold. She looked around the spacious area for a few seconds. It appeared to me she didn't like the room or it reminded her of her old lifestyle. I remember being at the Simmons mansion and thinking it cost a pretty penny. She's used to this type of high-end living. "This is where you will be staying until your son comes for you. I don't know how long it will be, so make yourself feel at home. Go crazy if you want, tear some shit up, I don't give a damn. It's been a wild month, let me tell you. I'll be back with some food and water." She walked toward the bed and ran her hands gently across the soft fabric. "Wine." What the fuck, she spoke. "I drink wine."

Chapter 43
INVENTORY

Snake opened the car door, got in, and slammed it shut. Bam looked at him. Something was off and not to mention. The stitch coming off his body didn't smell right. Very fruity, he thought. "Are you ok?" Snake gave off a feeling of paranoia. "I'm good, I'm good." He sat the backpack on the backseat. He searched through his clothes for the car keys. He went in the same pockets multiple times unable to find them. He paused in mid-thought. Where the fuck did I put the keys? "What are you doing?" Bam said confused. What is his problem? "I'm looking for the keys." Snake continued to search his pockets. "They're in the ignition." Bam caught eye contact with Snake. His eyes were red and low, two signs of being high, plus the smell. Snake looked at the keys. Damn, I just made a complete fool of myself. He knows I'm high. He brought his attention up to Bam. The look on his face was serious and goofy.

He giggled unable to help himself. "You're a fucking idiot." Bam understood the situation. "Did you at least double-check if you got everything we came for?" That's one thing that can't go wrong. His money is more important than anything. Snake turned his attention to the road. He put the car in drive. "Relax, everything is in the bag." This was his moment to be cool. Fuck what Bam thinks about me. They arrived at the mansion fifteen minutes later. Snake turned the car off and exhaled. He felt Bam staring at the side of his face. He turned to his attention. "What?" Bam smirked. "Grab the bag." He got out the car leaving no chance for Snake to respond. That's how he wanted it to be in the end. No chance. "Uncool," Snake said in a relaxed fashion. He grabbed the backpack off the back seat and entered the house. He heard Bam shouting for Abel from the hallway. He entered the living room. Abel appeared over the guardrail of the stairs. "Bam, there's no need to shout my name over and over again." He eyed him as he walked down. Bam watched Abel as he approached. There was something about the way he stared at him. He tried not to panic as he towered over him. Abel grabbed Bam by the chin and nearly crushed his jaw bone. "Do you have what I asked for?" Snake smirked. He enjoyed every second of Bam's agony. Bam struggled to move his jaw to speak. Abel is very strong. Why is he doing this to me? Gina, that bitch. Abel had never been aggressive with him. He was finally free from the deathlock. "Snake went in." He massaged his jaw. "Everything is in the backpack." Abel smirked. "Thank, you." He patted Bam on the shoulder. Gina convinced him to make Bam pay for how he spoke to her. They had passionate sex after Snake and Bam left the house. Gina's pussy is manipulative. He easily fell under her control. Snake reached his arm out with the bag in his hand. He didn't have to say anything. After Abel took it, they made eye contact. He wasn't high anymore. Abel gave him a certain look that made him feel unsure. Maybe he could smell the weed on him? He contemplated if he should say anything to ease the tension. "I smell like weed, don't I?" Abel didn't say anything but raised his eyebrow in speculation. "Unfortunately, the entire apartment smelt this way." Snake tried to sound innocent. "I was unaware of your brother being a pothead." Kane smoking weed is at the bottom of his problems. Abel checked the bag. The black notebook was there with the yearbook. No laptop. "You didn't find the laptop?" He strapped the backpack around his shoulder. Snake wanted to avoid any excuses. He forgot the laptop and that was unacceptable. He's smart enough to know when Abel was testing him. "I fucked up." "At least you brought back the notebook. I'm sure Kane has an ideal I murdered our father. We'll have to kill him." Abel walked towards the living room. He wasn't that concerned about the laptop. Kane will never crack the passcode. The notebook is worth seven hundred million and his future. The only delay is finding where his father hid the money and supply. Snake followed behind Abel. "He will know you're coming after noticing the bag is missing." He didn't think it was a good idea to murder his entire family. The cops would be all over them. "Kane won't do anything about it." Abel stood in the living room, looking in the notebook. "My brother is soft. He's been that way his entire life." Bam was observing while holding his jaw in pain. He watched Gina appear over the balcony. Soon, very soon. Gina held a smirk after making eye contact with Bam. Bam nodded slowly assuring her of his revenge. The conversation developing in the room regained his attention. Entertaining her will momentary be on hold. "He hit the museum like a Mack Truck." Snake got the attention of Abel. "He won't lay down." Abel shut the book with enough force the sound echoed. "So, he grew some balls for one night." He got close enough to breathe on Snake's forehead. The one-time Kane decided to show some balls, Snake throws it in his face. He was disgusted with himself after the museum heist. His knucklehead brother outsmarted him, not once, but twice. The other time was when he took the notebook from the house. "I'm only recommending that keeping Kane alive is beneficial, for now." He locked eyes with Abel. "Your father, the girl, and your brother. It'll look like either you or your mother pulled the trigger on Jar Simmons. We don't want any detectives sniffing around when we're trying to achieve the ultimate goal we planned back at school." Abel gave Snake room to breathe. Simple thinking, this is why Snake is second in command. Focus on the mission, then commit, follow by executing. He agreed. "I want to go over every location Jar visited that is documented in this book." He paused to lower his voice only for Snake to hear. "There's a possibility Jar kept a hidden inventory at one of the locations." "I thought the money was being held in a private bank account under the alias, Bill something..." Snake maintained his cool while speaking quietly. "The money is only half the business." He told him. The other half came to him after hearing about the African army raining down on the police. That scenario made him think about where the Africans got their weapons. "They don't accept guns in bank accounts."

Chapter 44
NEW MEMBER -KANE-

Smoke was right about Jimmy Tang. He cracked the passcode which could solve my father's murder. DIE KANE in all caps. Does that mean I'm my brother's next victim? "You did it." I stood next to Jimmy in front of the laptop. "No doubt." Jimmy sounded confident. Cracking the code was a piece of cake. "So... whatever you're looking for has to be important." He said from behind me. "You don't want to involve yourself in this situation." I heard Smoke informing Jimmy. "This shit is deep. Trust me." I was staring at the computer. Smoke is absolutely right about what he just said. I turned around to face them both. "Tang, Smoke was trying to warn you. This situation is complicated, but I really could use your help. Before you answer." I looked at Smoke for conformation. His expression told me he was good. "What we're involved in can get you killed." "I'm down," Tang answered swiftly. "I didn't get a chance to tell you…" He cut me off. "Fuck it, I'm down dude. Don't try to convince me otherwise." Tang answer with a serious look on his face. "I don't care what it is. My entire life has been doing what my father told me to do. I don't want to be stuck here forever. I know about your father and Redd. I watch the news. I also know you didn't murder the teacher." He paused. "I was there when your brother took the bat from your locker. I feel like a bitch for not saying anything. I wasn't sure at the time if he did it or not. I just want to help. I owe it to you." Tang reminded me that the last two years of my life had been pure hell. The surprising bit of information was that he saw my brother take the bat from my locker. And… didn't say shit. My bad side told me to at least break his nose. Somehow, my good side agreed. "Ok, you're in." I held out my hand. "Wait, just like that?" Tang sounded unsure. "I'm in?" "Just like that, you're in." I looked at Smoke. "He's good, right?" "At least I know you won't snitch." Smoke looked at Tang. "He's in." He held his hand out with a serious look on his face. "Shit," Tang pounded his fist in his hand. "I'm in. I wanted to be down with you guys for so long. Since like, third grade. You guys didn't even recognize me. I was nobody. But, now." He started breathing hard. "Now, I'm the shit. Nobody can stop me…" Smoke and I looked at each other like, who did we just invite into our circle? Tang went on and on about a bunch of nonsense. He wasn't going to stop anytime soon. "I'm the mothafucking man now." Tang was hype. "My father can kiss my a..." "Jimmy, Jimmy, Jimmy." I signed with my hands. "Chill, my man. It's all good, but you have to act the part of the crew. That means no crazy shit. Calm, cool, and collective is the best way to be, understood?" "I got you." Tang calmed down. "I do want to know how I can die from squadin' up with the crew. What type of shit are you guys in? The room is soundproof. Nobody can hear on the outside. You're good." "The African army killed Redd and we have a diamond they desperately want." I saw the expression on his face change. "I'm sure my brother murdered my father. That's why I needed the passcode for the laptop. He's also after the diamond. We were set up by The Planner, who's a crooked FBI agent." "I don't believe you two dum..." Tang checked himself. "I mean, smart guys stole that diamond from the museum. It's all over the news. No way, I don't believe you. I want you to show me." "Hell, no." Smoke spoke up. "Now you sound like a snitch." "Jimmy," I wanted to make one thing clear. "I don't trust you enough right now. It's your choice to be down with us. I'm only making you aware of the situation." "Why do you need me?" Tang looked back and forth between Smoke and I. "I can't fight the fucking African army. Your brother is another story. I've never slapped a pussy and your brother isn't one. He's... a... fucking... murder... er." "I need you because you're smart, dumbass." I told him. "You wanted to be down with us, remember? I don't expect you to be a tough guy. If I have you working on stuff for me. You need to know what you're getting involved in. Starting with this." I moved to the side so he could see the laptop. "I need you to scan this computer for anything that mentions my father." "I got you." Tang smiled. "We'll drop by tomorrow afternoon." I told him. "Jimmy, I'm trusting you with this laptop. If anything happens to it." Tang interrupted. "I know. You'll cut my balls off and hand dem to me, potna." Smoke and I had awkward looks on our faces. "No, fool. Smoke, what's up with your man? What I was about to say is I won't have another way of finding out if my brother did murder our father. This is all the evidence I have so be careful." "Right," Tang said. "I'll be done by tonight. But after that, I want to do some gangsta shit. I can't be stuck in the lab being the smart guy." "But that's what you do." Smoke said nonchalantly. "You're the smart one unless you rather pull up and drop them Africans who murdered our boy. That's always an option." I smirked. Tang had a scared look on his face. Tang is like one hundred and twenty pounds. He'll give his left nut, not to take on any kind of army. "I think I'll stay in the lab for now." Tang played it cool. "It's where my genius is needed." "It's yours." I handed Tang the laptop. "We'll see you tomorrow."

"Check you manana." Smoke followed behind. "It's mingtian, fool." Tang said in his language. "I don't speak, Chinese." Smoke shut the door behind us.

Chapter 45
INTRUDER -KANE-

Smoke unlocked the car and I got in the passenger side. I felt a little guilty for involving Tang. My father told me, I'm only as good as the people I'm surrounded by. My brother is smart and so is his team. They all went to school together. If he did commit the murder, then there's a chance he'll come for me or our mother. If I'm gonna take him out, I'll need people who think like him on my team. "Thanks." "For what?" Smoke started the car and strapped on his seat belt. "For being my brother." Smoke had done a lot for me in the past month. Some things were outrageous, like the bank robbery and museum heist. Not to mention, Ke'Mo Cutt. You would have thought he was blood after going through pure havoc and sticking around for me. "Having my back through all this drama." I sighed. "There's a chance we can die." "Then we'll die together." Smoke faced me. "I only dreamed of having ten million dollars. You made that happen. After I dropped that kid, there wasn't any turning back. My grandmother told me to finish what I start. Good or bad, I'm here." He held out his fist. I smiled and gave him some dap. "My brotha." "Alright, enough with all this sensitive stuff." He backed the car out from the parking lot. "Where we headed?" "Let's get some food and head back to the crib. I need to get ready for tonight." "Oh, yeah." Smoke turned to the corner. "You're visiting Kim later, I forgot. Kiss her for me." "I will." Smoke went through the drive-thru of Big Burgers. We got our food and headed towards the apartment. I grabbed my food and got out. "You know what I've been meaning to ask you?" Smoke shut the car door. "What's that?" I said while walking up the stairs. I unlocked the door and went in. Smoke followed. "Is everything cool with Bear? That's a lot of bread he's sitting on." I sat the food on the table and took off my shades. Smoke sat on the couch where he was before leaving the apartment. "Bear is fine." I grabbed the burger from the bag. "He hasn't spent a dime. He wants to move out of his mother's house." I ate one of the fries. Salty but good. "Right," Smoke sounded cool about it. "This is an enormous fucking burger." My pocket lit up, followed by a ringing sound. The name that appeared on the screen surprised me. I heard Smoke asked in the background for the remote control to the TV. "Look inside of the couch." I answered the call. "Rick." "Kane, are you ok?"

Rick sounded uneasy. "If you're talking about Jordan. I haven't heard from him." Smoke found the remote. I took a big bite out of the burger. "I know." Rick sounded assuring. "I want to tell you this before you hear about it on the news." I stopped chewing and swallowed everything in my mouth. This is going to be bad. My first thought, something happened to Kim. Gina went after her again. Possibly something good like they caught The Planner. "I received a call in the middle of the night, an officer was murdered and a woman was kidnapped." Rick paused. "I hate to do this to you after what you have already been through. The woman who was kidnapped was Noti Simmons." "What." It wasn't a question. I understood perfectly. My mother was kidnapped in the middle of the night from Hill Heights. An officer was killed in the line of duty. This happened because of me, what I've done. Abel, The Planner, and the African army all want my head. I took millions from the Africans and soon they'll find out the diamond is fake. The Planner wants the money. I'm in this situation because of him. My brother is a murderer, I'm beginning to think he would do anything to get this notebo... I look towards the couch. The backpack wasn't there anymore. I'm positive I put it there before we left to meet Jimmy Tang. "We have a description of the suspect and video footage." Rick told me. "The guy wore a hat and a long overcoat. It's hard to tell who, but I have a general idea." I interrupted. "It's not Jordan." I hung up the phone. This is personal. I noticed Smoke staring at me with a serious look on his face. "The bag is gone. Abel broke into the apartment while we were gone." What was going on with Smoke? Didn't he hear what I just said? The sound coming from the TV caught my attention. It was the news. The headline read, Officer Murdered in Hill Heights Kidnapping. Smoke found out my mother had been kidnapped. She was named as the missing person. I wasn't thinking about food anymore. I sat on the couch across from him. I focused on the news as did he. They didn't have much information on the suspect. The video footage hadn't been released. I didn't need it, my brother did this because I had evidence against him. Gina went after Kim and that didn't work. He went after the diamond and somehow figured out I was with the opposition. Is murdering our mother worth what he's after? This is bigger than the diamond. He needs my mother to figure out my father's network. Maybe he wants to trade her for the laptop? Whatever is on it means that much to him. "Whatever you want to do, I'm down." Smoke said seriously. "The bag is gone." I repeated. "There isn't anything else out of place. Abel knew I took it." At that moment I didn't think about the twenty-three million and the diamond stashed in my room. "Shit." I jumped up and hurried to the bedroom. I heard Smoke shouting in the background, what's up? If the money's gone, there's no way I can help my mother or Kim. The diamond is another problem. I opened the closet. I reminded myself to breathe slowly to calm down. The suitcase is where I left it. The diamond was still hidden and untouched. I shut the closet door. That could've made things worse. That's conformation Abel only came for the backpack. That eliminates The Planner and the Africans. I walked into the living room. Smoke was standing, ready to discuss our next move.

Chapter 46
LET'S DANCE -JORDAN-

Isat in a chair next to Mrs. Simmons in the room. We were drinking the finest wine, courtesy of the don. There's been a sudden change in her. I thought she was mute based on the information I've read. Her husband's death supposedly drove her insane. She hasn't been in the right state of mind for a few months. What pisses me off is I went through the trouble of being cautious with her. Now, it seems to me everything is working upstairs. I have to pick her brain to find out what she knows. If she gives me trouble, I'll have to get in contact with Kane before I kill her. Getting my money back is the main priority. "You can speak all of a sudden?" "I've been able to speak my entire life." She took a sip of her wine. "Is that a problem?" "We'll see," I looked back at her devilishly. The game has just begun. I cut straight to the point. "Where were you thirty minutes ago?" Simple question. She got up and wandered around the room. I studied her movements. That's me being a detective. I didn't get an immediate answer. Stalling, trying to figure me out and come up with something that will get her out of this predicament. That's not gonna work, Mrs. Simmons. "I was at home, where you came to get me." She stopped at the window and looked out into the world. "I don't remember much. Everything up there is scrambled." I thought about what she was saying. Her memory was slowly coming back. I read her file before going rogue. She's suffering from amnesia. She picked the perfect time to start remembering shit. "Home, by that you mean Hill Heights?" She smiled for the first time. "Is that the name of that awful place?" She sounded sarcastic while walking towards the center of the room. "Where is my son, Abel?" That question took me by surprise. The look on her face was serious. Abel? Who gives a fuck where he's at? I can't stand that kid. I had to visit Abel during the murder investigation of his father. Being in his presence gave me the chills. "Don't have a clue, maybe he's at the house or back at school." She had a sour look on her face and it sounded like she muttered, I doubt it. "Let's focus for a minute. Do you know who I am?" "Yes." She wasn't facing me when she said it. She walked over to the wine table and poured another drink. I'm glad I didn't have my gun on me at the time. I wanted to shoot her in the face when she said, yes. She knows who I am, does it matter? I had to ask myself that before

I committed to something foolish. The world knows I'm a bag guy by now, it's obvious. Rick will come after me no matter what. It doesn't make a difference. "Who am I?" "Some guy name The Planner." Suddenly, she laughed. "I'm sorry for laughing, but that's the name you told me. What kind of name is, The Planner? Who are you supposed to be, an evil villain or something? You look like a cop to me." Ok, now she really pissed me off. How dare this bitch laugh at my name? When I get my money from Kane, they're both dead. It was hard keeping my composure, she gave me a valid reason to blow her head off her shoulders. I could do that, but bad guys like me know how to make every predicament work in their favor. "I am a cop, The Planner is my code name. I'm undercover working the murder investigation of your husband. I had to extract you from Hill Heights for your safety." "Bullshit." Mrs. Simmons sat in the chair next to me. "I can tell when someone is lying to me. Tell me the truth. Why do you need me? I don't see any other cops around here. Unless you guys are cutting back on security?" Smarter than I thought. "Your son, Kane. He's a criminal and I thought by bringing you here would create some leverage. We know that he visits you at the hospital four times a week. There's no doubt he'll be looking for you. I want to use you to get him to turn himself in. If he feels like you're unsafe, he'll have no other choice." I laid it down for her without telling the whole truth. Hopefully, that'll be enough information for her to bite. It took her a second to process the information about her son. "My son is not a criminal. He wasn't raised that way. Tell me, what has he done for the police to be after him?" She crossed her legs. She appeared more confident and relaxed than before this conversation started. "Since the death of your husband." A little truth doesn't hurt. I am the reason why Kane jumped into a life of crime. "Your son and some of his friends robbed Westwood Bank. That led to them stealing a diamond from the Atlanta museum. We, meaning the department, have been trying to catch him ever since. It could be the murder of his father or living in jail for the past two years contribute to making these decisions." "My son did all that?" She laughed. "Kane isn't that type of boy. Maybe Abel, but not my son, Kane. He's a good child." "Your son has about fifty million dollars of the government's money." I told her. I was stern when I said it. Mrs. Simmons was beginning to frustrate me. Her pride for Kane was made her believe he's incapable of committing those crimes. "Sounds like fifty million dollars of your money." She smiled before sipping her wine. Enough is enough. She's playing me. I'm a fool for not believing she doesn't know who I am. I don't need anything from her so why am I entertaining this conversation? I'm better than this and it's time to show her whose boss. "I tried to kill your son. The fifty million dollars was a set up by me. I'm a dirty cop and currently on the run. That's why I kidnapped you from the hospital. He outsmarted me after stealing the diamond, it's that simple. He used my partner against me. The only way I'll get my money is to trade you for it. After that, I plan to kill him and you for my troubles." I gulped the last of the wine and set the glass on the table. Noting changed about her demeanor. "I have a better proposition. Take me to Africa and I can promise you one hundred million dollars. And Kane is off-limits, Mr. Jordan."

Chapter 47
AFRICA

Abel sat at his father's desk studying the notebook. He discovered that his father was doing something that made a lot of money a year ago. Smuggling guns to rebels wasn't at the top of his list. That didn't matter to him, all he wants is money and power. Continuing to smuggle weapons is out of the question, but clearing out the remaining supply is another thing. The only problem is finding out where Jar kept his secret inventory. Whenever there is a situation that puts you at risk of a life sentence. You will need a secret safe house that doesn't require a bank account. Something that will lift you in the end if all else fails. That's what he's searching for, seven hundred million would easily solve all of his problems. "Where did you hide it old man?" He lit a cigarette and relaxed in the chair. He put his hand on top of his head to message his brain cells. The notebook was driving him crazy. He thought about forcing the information out of his father before murdering him. That would've been the intelligent thing to do at the time. He closed the book to start over. I'm overthinking, he thought. Time to hit the reset button. He scanned the first page. South Asia, his father smuggled millions of weapons in the country. The numbers were outrageous. He flooded a ton of weapons to India and Pakistan. What are the possibilities of having an inventory in a high demand area? If it was me, I wouldn't chance of having my inventory there, too high of a risk. He flipped the page. Europe, several pages covered the United Kingdom. Germany and France were in the lead for the most imports and exports. Jar made a lot of money selling small arms and light machine guns in those places. A few pages ahead, he found the Kalashnikov AK-47, which was the most popular weapon sold because of its low cost. He turned the page, Africa. He stared at the page skeptically. Something was wrong. On all of the other pages, there were costs, weapons, exports, and imports. He got up from the seat. His father had a large map on the wall in his office. Jar rarely used this office because he stayed away from home. Abel stood in front of the map, studying Africa. He blew out a ring of smoke. Africa, why didn't I see this before? He heard a knock at the door. "Come in." Gina entered the room. "Is everything ok?" She closed the door and walked to the center of the room. She didn't want to enter Abel's space without permission. She knew how he could be when he was deep in thought. "Yes." Short answer. Libya, he thought. "You have been up here for hours." She took a step forward, wanting to be close to him. If there was anything she could do to help solve his problem, she would do it without question. "I made you a sandwich." Her voice was soft and innocent. Never had she made a sandwich for any other man in her life, not even her father. The only thing she'll put over money is her love for Abel. Abel didn't respond, his focus was clearly on the map. Gina felt unwanted after a few seconds. Abel didn't pay her any mind. Deep down, he hurt her feelings. She only wants his love to be true as her love is for him. Her emotions began to take over and her eyes became watery. She sat the sandwich on the table and hurried towards the door. She reached for the doorknob. "Thank you." Abel caught Gina before the threshold. There is a small place in his heart for her. She is the only person that made him feel a certain way about a woman. He thought it was because of sex. It wasn't that at all, his feeling for her grew past pleasure. She's everything he wants in a woman, a murderous genius that's equivalent to his own mind. She froze at the door, hand on the knob ready to exit. Although, Abel didn't let her go without recognizing her efforts. Heartache isn't good for any human being who wants to be loved. "You're welcome." "Don't leave, stay." Abel walked to the table and picked up the sandwich. "I want to explain to you what I've been doing all this time." He took a bite of the sandwich. "You're studying the notebook." Gina took her hand off the doorknob. She turned to face him. "Did you find what you're looking for?" The sandwich was amazing. Half of the meal was gone. Feeding his hunger gave him a boost of energy. He felt alive again. He set the plate on the table and walked to Gina. "Come, let me show you." He reached for her hand and interlocked with hers. He guided her to the map on the wall. Gina's other hand covered the slight small on her face. Their hands locked together made her feel desirable. They stopped in front of the map. Gina noticed push pins on certain locations. "These are the areas your father smuggled weapons?" "Yes and no." He watched a confused look transform on Gina's face. "Let me explain. The red pins are hostile, white pins are natural, the yellow pins are landing strips. Jar tracked the behavior of each place he traveled to and their landscape. The reason behind his tactic is simple. He needed a central location for a headquarters." "I'm estimating around twenty red pins." Gina faced the map and pointed to each location while speaking. "Thirty white and five yellow. Wait a second..." She noticed something peculiar. "All of the yellow push pins are in Africa, and it appears to only be one green pin in Libya." Abel smiled. "Exactly, the notebook corresponds with the map.

There's a section on Africa that only shows locations, fuel stations, arrival time, warehouses, and contacts. Libya is where my father's base of operation is located. Africa is the perfect continent to have a headquarters for trafficking. The infrastructure is great and includes a landing strip for both importation and exportation. The warehouses provide storage for products waiting for delivery. The headquarters is somewhat a central location near each customer. Multitudes of unoccupied land used to traffic product." "Your father was a genius." Gina awed at the map looking at all of the locations. "How will you find the exact location of the headquarters?" "The land is corrupt, my father knew officials could either be bribed or blackmailed." Abel explained. "A lax financial system provides security so that large amounts of money can be moved without looking suspicious." "So, the government is watching over the headquarters?" Gina asked curiously. "Not exactly." Abel backed away. He approached the table and picked up the last of his sandwich. He grabbed the black notebook and walked back to her. "Take a look at this." He took a bit of the sandwich while watching Gina study the notebook. After a few seconds, Gina found what she was looking for. "The African army was helping your father." She said quietly with barley enough volume for him to hear. "But, who is the primary contact?" Abel smiled. "That's simple. The General." "How do you position yourself with the leader of the African army?" She asked. "You're not Jar." "I think a black diamond will solve that problem." Abel took the last bit of the sandwich. "Delicious."

Chapter 48
MY TWIN -KANE-

"I think my brother kidnapped our mother." I told Smoke. I came to the decision it was him. "A, The Planner wouldn't have wanted a backpack with a laptop and a notebook in it. He would've come for the diamond or the money. B, the Africans would've made a mess. And there's a slim chance they know where I live and about my mother. The Hummer is parked outside, but it doesn't have an apartment number on it. Abel is the only person who would've come for the bag. I took it from the house and he assumed it was me. He was correct. The notebook was in it." "But why would he kidnap his mother if he got the notebook back?" Smoke asked. "And he could just visit her if he wanted to ask any questions about the book." "No, my mother can barely speak or comprehend anything I say." I told him. "I doubt she can explain anything to him. Not after what she told me. She knows he murdered my father. It would've been difficult for Abel to speak with her without commotion. He doesn't want to kill her because that could've been done in her sleep. He needs her for something." "What do you think it is?" Smoke appeared to be deep in thought. "Honestly, it could be anything." I thought about the situation before I answered. "I'm thinking he didn't check the bag before he left. He realized the laptop was missing after it was too late. There could be something on there that ties him to my father's murder. Trade mom for the laptop. My second thought, there is something in the notebook he doesn't understand. There is a possibility my mother knew about the book and my father. Finally, good old revenge. Threatens to murder her if I don't give him the laptop and the diamond." "He figured out it was us?" Smoke said. "Your brother is crazy as fuck. I never thought that smart mufucka would turn out to be a killer. Whatever it takes, we'll get her back." "I don't know," I answered honestly. I thought about the question a moment longer. What will I do? It's a simple solution if all he wants is the diamond or the laptop. I'll do anything for my mother. If it came down to murdering my brother, I will. "I'm not sure if he actually murdered our father until Jimmy gets us the information off the laptop. I'm sure about the museum, the girl, his friend kidnapping Kim, and the notebook." "I think it's time to confront your brother." Smoke said, seriously. "Obviously, something is going on. We can't wait for Jimmy." Before I could respond, my phone rang. I answered it without looking at the caller ID. I'm sure it's Rick, calling back after I hung up the line. "Kane." "I know you have the diamond." A harsh voice came through the receiver. This is unbelievable. My blood instantly set on fire. I wanted to teleport through the phone. This was our fate. Born together to become enemies. "Abel." My heart began to beat rapidly. I was right, he wants the diamond. I'm eighty percent sure he murdered my father. I heard him breathing through the phone. "The diamond, brother." I have a feeling he's smiling on the other end. "I know about father." That's all I had to say. I wanted him to know. I can't fuck around any longer. Smoke, Bear, and Redd are my brothers. Our commitment to each other is something I never had with Abel. "And why did you kidnap our mother?" Abel's breathing increased. He didn't respond. "You didn't think I would find out the shit you did?" I needed to get this off my chest. "I know about everything. Tell me different?" Again, silence. I only heard him breathing. Smoke caught my attention. I read his lips, he did that shit. Abel doesn't have to answer me. I'm at my boiling point. I can't wait to see T-Mac and Big Bruce. There's a bed in prison with my name on it. Abel decided to become my enemy the day we were born. He has to die. "Is that why you sent Gina to murder Kim? You don't have to answer that. I found out about your little psychopath girlfriend in the yearbook." I paused so he could take everything in. I watched Smoke nod his head. He knows what time it is, war. "I'll bring the fucking diamond. Get my mother ready." The line went dead. I told Abel what he wanted to hear. After my mother is safe, he's dead. I can't let it end any other way. I put the phone in my pocket. I looked at Smoke. "We strappin' up?" He lifted his shirt revealing a gun on his waist. I nodded slowly as an answer. Smoke kept a gun on him after what happened with the Africans. I don't blame him. I'm at war with Abel. Strappin' up is a priority. He will try to kill me the first chance he gets. It's no surprise after what he's done. Who would expect to be in a circumstance like this within their family? Abel did this to us. I don't need a plan. He's at the house. "Call Bear, make sure he's strapped. Abel is expecting us to pull up." I went to the bedroom. There's a chance I can die. Abel is prepared to kill me, just like that. I'm nothing to him. He's nothing to me. I opened the closet door and slid the suitcase to the side. I grabbed one of the shoe boxes on the top shelf. The day Kim and I went to the museum should've been the last day. The diamond has been nothing but trouble. Something I didn't ask for. I just wanted a job. I put the diamond in a handbag and strapped it around my shoulder. I grabbed a Desert Eagle out of the same box. I put on a black jacket after holstering the gun on my waist. I stepped out of the closet and shut the door. My enemy was staring back at me in the mirror. The person I convince myself to kill, My Twin.

Chapter 49
DETAIL

"Damn," Rick said. Kane hung up the phone without giving him a chance to explain. "This is beginning to be frustrating." Trying to figure out Jordan's next move had taken a toll on his brainpower. He hates to admit things were a lot easier when Jordan was his partner. Two minds are better than one any day. The department has yet to assign him a new partner. For now, he's solo. Jordan won't be easy to bring down, he's a street cop. Jordan is like Denzel in Training Day and he's Simon in Hot Fuzz. Two different types of mentalities. Rick sat in the car, deep in thought. Kane doesn't think it was Jordan. Rick believes the suspect is his former partner, Kane disagrees. If not, who does he think kidnapped his mother? This would be catastrophic if there's another suspect. Kane possibly held information about the diamond sting. He got out of the car and closed the door.

The parking lot is normally empty around noon. He counted about 50 police vehicles. Jordan's capture could propel a mid-tier officer to the next level. Make no mistake, Kane has his undivided attention. The feeling of Kane's connection with Jordan is important. The victim is his mother, Mrs. Simmons. His former partner was particularly after the kid, which told him something important. Rick entered the police department. Everyone in the building was trying to find Jordan's hideaway. He scanned the room. Officers were watching video footage, at the whiteboard, and conversing about evidence. His eyes stopped on a particular object, a desk. No one thought about searching Jordan's workstation. He casually began walking, not wanting to bother anyone. He thought about the time when they worked on the museum case. Jordan had turned on the department back then, using the information they gathered to steal the diamond. The Africans, Jordan, the kids, and the diamond are all connected. He pulled the chair out and stood behind the desk. A lock secured the right drawer. Dammit, he thought. That has to be the one. He sat in the seat and reached in his pocket. Hopefully, this won't get him in trouble. He secretly held the lock pick low in his hand. His eyes were scanning the room. No one cared about what he was doing, as almost to not give a damn. He nonchalantly began to pick the lock. It took him a few seconds before he heard a click. He pulled back on the handle. A row of manila file folders appeared in alphabetical order. Every case they had worked together was in the drawer. His fingers ran across the folders. Only two caught his interest. The name tag on the first folder read, Jar Simmons. He sat it on top of the desk and then reached the second. When he began the pull it from the drawer, another folder grabbed his attention. He released the second folder and it slid back in place. He pulled out the third folder, Abel Simmons. Why would Jordan need a specific folder for Abel? The one-time Jordan wasn't himself was when they went to visit Mrs. Simmons at their mansion. Abel was there that day. There wasn't anything strange about the kid to him. He opened the file on Abel. His photo covered the first page. Both eyes were scratched out of the image. That's interesting. He turned the photo over and read the next page. It was a short report on Abel's interrogation after his high school teacher was murdered. His first case on the job at the department. Jordan was his partner. A part of Abel's statement caught his attention. My brother did it. He murdered my teacher. Jordan had collected the statement from another officer. Why would his brother say that? Rick didn't know anything about Jordan investigating Abel. The next page was an observation. He repeatedly read, genius, quiet, and monster. That's how Jordan described Abel. Monster? He also wrote, Abel was born a monster. He continued. A summary of the kidnapping was on the next page. Kane's girlfriend Kim was the victim. Rick sat back in the chair. The kid in the accident was connected to Abel. Alfred Ben went to the same school, he knew that. He sighed, something was missing. Mrs. Simmons was kidnapped by Jordan. Abel was involved in the museum heist. The Planner used Kane and Abel. That's the connection. Rick opened the museum folder. He found a particular image of a vent covered in bullet holes. Someone was shooting at the vent. He began piecing everything together, trying to make sense of it all. Kane told him he found the diamond on Ke'Mo. At the time, it didn't catch his attention. Ke'Mo was a profession hitman, not a thief. Kane had the diamond the entire time. Ke'Mo was sent to kill him. Jordan manipulated Kane and Abel steal the diamond. He gave them the blueprint. Kane escaped with the diamond. Abel decided to Kidnap Kim and got his friend killed. Kane never gave his brother up. He thinks Abel kidnapped their mother. Rick settled on Abel as the new bad guy. The connection between Jordan and the twins is real. Rick closed the folders and took them with him. Kane sounded convincing when they were on the phone. He hurried out of the building trying to save time. A strong gust of wind caught him at the door. He looked up at the sky. It was beginning to get dark outside. Thick clouds formed over his head and tiny drops of rain hit his face. Jordan was now second on his agenda. Kane is number one. The kid was about to do something that would land him back in jail. Rick opened the car door. He tossed the file folders in the passenger seat. The Simmons residence. He GPS the stop and started the car. That's where Kane will go looking for his brother. He reversed the car out of the parking space. His foot held the pedal to the floor. The windshield wipers fought hard against the aggressive rainfall. He checked the time, twenty minutes away from the location. He thought about the chance of arriving late. He reached for his cell phone and called Kane. No answer. "Damn." He slammed his fist against the steering wheel.

Chapter 50
BANG, BANG -KANE-

Smoke and I left the apartment and met Bear at the bottom of the steps. He had on all black like he was ready to commit another bank robbery. I gave him some pound. "You ready?" "Didn't know I would need a strap to visit your brother." Bear patted the side of his waist. "But I'm good." "Neither did I." I led the way to the parking lot. "What's going on?" Bear asked. "I'll let you know while we're on the way." Smoke unlocked the car and we got in. I strapped on the seat belt and got comfortable. I didn't want the hand cannon jammed in my side for the entire trip. I sat in the passenger seat and Bear got his big ass in the back. Deep down, I felt that this situation would get ugly. My fake brother doesn't mind putting a bullet in my head. How am I supposed to explain that to somebody? I elaborated to Bear what I recently discovered. He paid attention to everything I said and didn't fall asleep once. I finished with,

"He kidnapped my mother." I don't consider Abel my brother any longer. "I believe you," Bear said, convinced. "I'm down for whatever, even if we have to ride on your fake ass brother." "He's not my brother anymore," I spoke for both of them to understand. "You guys are." We were quiet for a moment. I was thinking about everything we had gone through up until this point. Smoke has been there since the beginning and Bear is proven. I don't know how I would get through this without them. I looked out of the window. The rain slapped hard against the windshield. I heard the wipers rapidly moving across the glass. The traffic was at a slow pace because of the weather. Smoke maneuvered around slower drivers. A storm is coming and it's not the rain. Abel will have to answer to me for everything he's done. I should've acted a long time ago when I was accused of murder. That teacher had a family and Abel took her away from them because of a damn grade. That's an evil sonovabitch that will do anything for self-interest. I reached inside the handbag and pulled out the diamond. This piece of shit ripped apart my family. I can't help but think Abel is somehow involved with the Africans. He sacrificed his family for money. Ironically, I thought Abel was smarter than that. "Would you murder your father for power?" The question was directed toward them both. I looked at them. Smoke appeared to be pondering an answer and Bear was doing the same. Abel committed that crime. I respected their decision not to answer. Therefore, I thought about killing Abel for the rest of the way. I set my mind to be at his level of insanity. The energy and emotion he gives off I will return with the same intensity. That's the only way to get my mother back safely. There's no time to be acting soft. We crept to a stop down the street. My parent's house was in view. "Turn off the car." I told Smoke while I unstrapped my seat belt. The rain was loud enough to hear it colliding with the car. I didn't see any activity at the house. I was beginning to wonder if Abel was even home. The lights were off and that made the place appear lifeless. I have a feeling Abel is waiting for me to arrive with the diamond. "The house looks deserted." Smoke spoke up. I turned to his attention. "He's there," I wanted to feel in control of the situation. Abel thinks he has more influence by calling and demanding the diamond. That's not the case, I'm the one giving orders. "Waiting for us to make a move. I can feel it. He wants me to make a mistake." "What about knocking on the door?" Bear chirped from the back seat. "What?" Smoke said with sarcasm. "I'm saying," Bear began. "We have guns like we're ready for war. There's a chance he just wants a clean swap. Who says there has to be a shootout? It's the afternoon. Just saying." Damn, I didn't think about it that way. What if Abel does want a swap without any problems? I wiped the thought from my mind. That's not gonna happen. I know him. First, he'll try to convince me to hand over the diamond. Second, he'll try to kill me if I don't. His way or no way. Doesn't matter if we're brothers or at the house in broad daylight. Abel lives by setting goals and making them a reality. "You're talking about the guy who shot you in the shoulder." "Damn," I heard the sarcasm in Smoke's voice. "That's right, he did shoot you in the shoulder." He looked back at Bear. "You still wanna knock on the door?" Bear grunted. "How you want to handle this?" Smoke asked. That's a good question. We all are large men, climbing through my bedroom window won't be an option. Bear is kind of right, but that could lead to a setup. We could kick in the front door and run in there like Rambo. Think. I looked up at my house and was taken by surprise. "Just call Abel." Smoke suggested but it was too late. I squinted my eyes to see through the rain. Smoke didn't have the wipers on so it was hard to see through the window. "I think Gina is outside." She was standing in the front yard. What the fuck is she doing? She has yet to look our way. It's hard to tell if she's aware of us or not. "Who?" Bear asked, confused. "Gina," Smoke told him. "The girl in the yearbook." "Yearbook?" Bear looked at me. "The naked girl from the museum." Smoke submitted. "Damn." "Oh," Bear said. I watched him smile after remembering the woman. "It's a long story." I turned my eyes on Gina. It was definitely her standing in the rain. "I found a yearbook when I broke into my house. There were pictures of Abel and his friends. The same friends from the museum." I paused to point at Gina. They followed my finger out the window. "And that bitch, right there, tried to kill Kim." "Got it, big guy? She's crazy." Smoke pulled out his gun. "There's only one way to do this." Bear pulled out his strap. "Bang, bang." "Chill," I held the gun in my hand. "No reason to have a shootout just yet. She doesn't look like she wants a war." I looked at the girl. "Although, she's crazy as hell, so be ready. I think she's waiting for us to pull up. Start the car and stop at the beginning of the driveway." The car began moving slowly. The moment felt like we were initiating a drive-by. I'm not down with killing a woman. I never imaged coming across one as savage as Gina. She's a monster and I'll drop her if need be. I cocked my weapon.

Chapter 51
NEW DEAL -JORDAN-

Africa? What is this woman talking about? I think Mrs. Simmons drunk too much wine. "You can promise me one hundred million dollars if I take you to Africa?" I began to laugh. She probably thinks I'm insane. "That sounds fucking crazy. Oh, I bet you want to know why?" I got up after growing frustrated. "I just kidnapped you from a fucking mental hospital!" I yelled. I knew sooner or later I would snap. I bent down close to her face. She appeared to be unfazed while staying put in the chair. She didn't even flinch. I stood up and backed away. "Sorry, sometimes I can be rude." I sighed and started for the door. "I'm telling you the truth." I heard her from over my shoulder. "Do you really think my husband was only working in real estate?" I stopped in my tracks. I remembered questioning Jar's income when I worked his case. The million-dollar mansion and the expansive cars were a dead giveaway. Two suspicious purchases involving large amounts of money. "What's in Africa?" "My husband's headquarters." She saw the look on my face. "He was a weapons trafficker. There is a safe in Libya and I know the passcode." "A smuggler?" I muttered. That took me by surprise. "I was on to your husband." "You wouldn't have discovered his secret." She told me. "He was a prominent member of Africa's Arms trade. The African army worked for my husband. If he supplied them with weapons, they protected his business." I thought about it for a moment. I can't go to Africa. Not after what went down with the diamond. This is more serious than I imagined. Jar was deep in the game. I won't stand a chance against the General. That's what I'm facing if I leave the country. I chose the perfect time to piss off the African Army. Damn, what a coincidence. "What type of headquarters?" "Several massive warehouses with a landing strip." She sipped her wine. "The property is claimed by the president so no one goes there or question its whereabouts. Soldiers patrol the property throughout the entire day." This conversation is getting interesting. Jar came up with a smart idea to hide his smuggling business. The land where the headquarters operates on is owned by the president. If the warehouses were discovered, the weapons wouldn't have led back to Jar. "Let me be honest with you. I rather get the fifty million dollars from your son and then kill you. It's easier," I nonchalantly shrugged my shoulders.

I don't think another 50 million is worth dealing with the Africans. "The money could be gone. I'm sure the Africans know your husband is dead. What if they took the money?" "It's in a secure place." She sounded confident. "I'm the only person who knows the exact location." I got angry. I stormed over to her and pointed at my chest while speaking. "If I'm going to risk-my-fucking-life, I need to know every-single-fucking-detail." I just ran out of patience. I need to shoot something. I pulled out my gun and aimed at a picture on the wall. BOOM! "You shot the baby?" She said ironically. I look at the picture on the wall. Damn, I did shoot the baby. The don's family photo of his wife holding their newborn child. "I didn't try to shoot the damn baby. It just happened," The look on her face told me she wasn't convinced. "Whatever, if you don't tell me precisely where the money is, you can forget about Africa." This woman sat there like a statue when the gun went off. She's not afraid of gunfire? A clear sign of being around guns. The mentally ill woman I kidnapped an hour ago turn into an OG. "It's in the ground under one of the warehouses." She elaborated for me. "Five years before my husband involved the African army. He bought land in Libya. His operation was growing fast. Africa was the perfect place for a headquarters. We lived there for five years. Every single day," She paused, memorized from remembering. "Jar would dig. He didn't trust anybody to do the work. Nobody could know about this place. My husband was a man of many trades. A secret place to hide all of our money. It's a specialized room to keep the money from decaying. After the job was complete, we hired workers to build five warehouses across the land. There's an available landing strip. We can fly there in a private plane." This sounds too good to be true. Although, I have a feeling she's telling the truth. My instinct always told me to stick to the plan. This is a tough decision. What to do? I lightly tapped the gun on the side of my head while thinking of the right move. How will I get us there without them filthy bastards knowing I'm in the country? Who do I know that owns a private plane? Fuck, my brother. I stepped closer to Mrs. Simmons and held out my hand. She gently shook it, accepting our alliance. "Deal."

Chapter 52
MAN UP -KANE-

Smoke stopped the car in front of the house. I studied Gina from my seat. She patiently stood in the rain. Her clothes were soaking wet. My eyes shifted to the house, searching for Abel. He could be using her as a distraction. I thought about the two guys in the photo with them. They'll be somewhere close, probably waiting for a signal. "I think we should get out." Smoke suggested. "I'm tired of waiting. Abel knows what it is. The diamond for your mother, simple." "Let's do it," Bear said. "There's no point sitting here like bait." "Ok," I agreed. "Be cautious of your surroundings when we get out of the car. You never know." I gripped the weapon. At this point, an ambush could come from anywhere. All we have to do is be ready. I put my hand on the door handle. They both moved accordingly. I pulled my hood over my head as I emerged from the vehicle. I shut the door and walked to the front of the car.

My boys stood next to me. We want them to know we're strapped. I held the gun down by my crotch. One hand over the over like a boss. I took a step forward. The diamond secured in my handbag. "Where is Abel?" I looked in her eyes. She didn't answer. "What's the deal with this chick?" Bear growled. "If you only knew." Smoke replied to the big guy. "I won't ask again." The guns didn't oppose any threat. There's no way she's scared. She's capable of anything, fearless. The threat is her, not us. Suddenly, she slowly held her hand out. I glanced at the sides of the house looking for trouble. That could've been a signal. "She's asking for the diamond." Smoke eyes were focused on Gina. "That's a fucked-up way to ask for something." Bear said. I opened the handbag and revealed the diamond. "You want this?" I held it up for her to see. The rain came down harder and the sound of thunder echoed in the sky. "My mother first." I watched an evil smile spread across her face. I spotted a large figure appear in the doorway. Abel. I felt a demonic presence when he emerged. Something was different about him. He stepped in the front yard. He didn't look armed with a weapon. His goon nerds followed him from the house. There wouldn't be any surprise attack. Both sides were staring down each other in an intense standoff. I stepped towards the center. My crew behind me, ready for whatever. I didn't have to speak. Abel met me in the middle. His crew behind him. When I punched him in the face, I didn't realize how much bigger he had gotten. We're close in height, but I'm more massive. Thanks to being incarcerated for two years. I stared into his devilish eyes and he smirked. "Hand over the diamond," he ordered without losing eye contact. "Our father?" I asked through cringed teeth. I was breathing heavily. Abel knows if he wants the diamond. He'll have to answer my question. "Why do you care?" He countered. "He left you in a rat hole for two years. He never really cared about our family. It was all about him. The lord of war, Jar Simmons." "He was our father," Abel's nonchalant attitude got me angry. "And you murdered him." I felt my hand squeezing the handle of the gun. I imagined a bullet flying in slow motion, striking him in the forehead. My eyes shifted off him to his crew. They appeared to be ready for work. "He was your father." Abel replied. "Imagine having twins and on their birthday, one of them was forgotten. The pain of having a father, but he only paid attention to one son. I'm sure you understand by now what I mean. I was the bad seed. No matter how smart I became, all of my efforts amounted to nothing." He smiled. "The only thing you had to do for attention was catch a football. Pathetic." "It's settled, you're a murderer." I wanted to get my mother to safety before I deal with Abel. I showed him the diamond. "Where's my mother?" "You won't find her here." He took a fighting stance. "I thought we would handle this the old-fashioned way and man up." He doesn't have her? I was wrong. Otherwise, why risk a fight when you can avoid conflict? Abel is smart, he tricked me into believing he kidnapped mom. Bastard. I locked on him, the look on his face was serious. Time up, he was prepared for battle. I turned to my crew. I handed my gun and the handbag to Bear. "If I lose, give him the diamond." "That won't happen." Bear said with confidence. "If shit gets ugly." Smoke motioned with his weapon. "I got you." I nodded. I turned to Abel's attention. Thunder roared in the sky. This fight is not just about my father. It's about every crime he has ever committed. I looked up at the sky through the harsh rainfall. I said a short prayer. Please don't stop me from killing my brother. I brought my eyes down on this monster. He wouldn't fight if he wasn't already prepared to get dirty. I can't underestimate him. We had never been in a fight against each other. I'll make sure this will be the last time. His eyes analyzed the competition. I'm bigger, he'll look for my weak spot. I put my hands up, balled fists. Everything around me turned black, tunnel vision. I began sizing him up, shorter, possibly faster, 40 pounds lighter, genius, and murderer. I fought Big Bruce, this doesn't compare. "I'll take it easy before I bury you like your worthless father." Abel closed in on me fearlessly. I didn't respond. He's trying to get in my head. I loaded up a death punch. He closed the distance between us even faster. I reacted by taking a shot at his head. I felt nothing but wind, I missed. What? He dodged my attack. The force behind the blow curried my body in an awkward direction. "Ah!" He countered by connecting with a blow to my stomach. Fuck, the pain was extraordinary. How did he learn to punch like that? It was the hardest punch I've ever felt. I dropped down to one knee. This can't be happening, it felt like his hand was made of steel. "I see you're trying to figure out what just happened." I heard his voice behind me. "It's amazing what you can learn in college. Self-defense was one of my majors. There's no way you can defeat me in a straight-up street brawl." Ok, that explains why he countered my attack. I'm dealing with a fighter. No, matter. I will win. I heard Smoke yell in the background, kick his ass! Bear followed by yelling out, get up! I picked myself up from the ground. My fists were up and ready. Abel stood in front of me in the same fighting stance as before. He moved in for another attack. I didn't swing this time. My face collided with his fist. I stumble back a bit before catching my balance. Fuck. He caught me with a surprise punch. The first time he's ever attempted something like that. I need to grab a hold of him. I know I'm stronger. He's too quick, trying to outbox him won't work. His skill is superior to mine. I need to get him on the ground and use my strength. "You're all muscle." He moved in slowly. "I'll bury next to the old man." "Finishing him, Abel!" I heard Gina call out in the background. I kept my eyes pinned on Abel. The scene became quiet. The only thing I could hear was the sound of rain hitting the ground. My vision became blurry after eating a shot to the face. My feet, legs, and arms suddenly got heavier. Abel moved closer. I anticipated another shot to the face. I dodge his attack successfully and connected with a powerful blow to his rib cage. He bent over and held his chest. I quickly wrapped my arms around his body. Before he had a chance to react, I suplexed him to the ground like a professional wrestler. The move had enough force behind it that water kicked up from the grass. I jumped to my feet just in case he recovered somehow unexpectedly. No movement in his body. I stood there not knowing if he had died. The suplex took a lot of my energy. The move could've broken his backbone. I turned my attention to his crew. They all had surprised facial expressions. "Abel!" Gina shouted his name frantically. "You sonofvabitch!" It was the guy from the yearbook. He took a step forward and Gina held out her arm to stop him. "Snake," Gina revealed his code name. "This is Abel's fight. He asked us not to interfere. Respect his rules." His real name was Samuel, I read it in the yearbook. I watched both of them. Snake appeared to be reluctant to help. The other guy stood there nonchalantly, I couldn't find his name in the book. He was only in that picture. He probably attended another school. He didn't show any signs of wanting to help Abel. It didn't matter to me. They all can get this work. "What are you waiting for?" Smoke voice echoed in the background. "Finish him." Smoke was right. I'm wasting too much time. I approached Abel. He laid face down on his stomach appearing to be lifeless. I cautiously grabbed the back of his shirt and powerfully lifted him from the ground. He was barely breathing. Good, I didn't want this to be over. He has to be punished for his crimes. I held him up with one hand. His eyes blinked open. He was regaining consciousness. Apparently, there wasn't anybody in his self-defense class with my size and strength. I wanted to wait for him to look me in the eyes. He deserves every bit of this ass whooping. Something unexpected happened. He slowly lifted his head. A sinister grin crossed his face. He was mocking me. I loaded up another attack with my right fist. I felt like Goku from Dragon Ball Z when he first became a Super Saiyan. I hit Abel with a Kamehameha punch that sent him flying. The shot propelled him into the air. He landed five feet away and slid to a stop next to Gina. I never hit anyone that hard. "You bastard!" It was Snake. He took a chance and rushed in my direction. "Snake!" Gina yelled, trying to stop him. It was too late. I didn't have to do anything. Bear caught him with a knockout blow just before he entered my space. The punch was devastating. His face turned awkwardly. After a few drunken steps in the wrong direction, he instantly dropped. I've never witnessed a punch like that ever in my life. I'm strong, but Bear is on another level. I wouldn't doubt he snapped his neck by the look of it. I nodded at Bear as to say, I got this from here, but thanks. He fell back into position. I turned my attention to the other guy. He didn't want any smoke after witnessing his buddy face get crushed. My vision had returned to normal. I thought I saw a smile on the other guy's face like he was enjoying watching his crew get their ass kicked. "Bam," I watched Gina attend to Abel. "Help Snake." She roared. Bam, that's a hell of a name. Now, I know the entire crew. Bam, Snake, Gina, and Alfred. They all have something to do with this by helping Abel. Bam didn't seem to care as much as the others. He was emotionless. He held his hands up as a sign of not trying to interfere. He watched us as he cautiously walked toward Snake. He was a lot smaller than the rest of their crew. I allowed him to help his counterpart. I only want Abel. Bam crouched down next to Snake. "He's asleep." "Get him inside the house." She ordered. "No." Bam stood. "I'm not strong enough. This is his fault. Abel warned him not to interfere." "It's not an option!" Gina shouted. "If something happens to Snake. Abel will kill us." What the hell is going on? Gina and Bam don't seem like they get along with each other. And Snake is probably Abel's best friend. He was in the majority of the photos with him. They must have a close relationship. Suddenly, I was distracted by a vehicle speeding up to a stop next to Smoke's car. A white man hopped out of the vehicle. "Ah!" I roared like a wounded lion. I was taken by surprise. I fell to my knees because the pain in my side was excruciating. A large arm wrapped around my neck. I began to choke. I held one hand on the arm and the other on my kidney area. I felt blood between my fingers. I had been stabbed. "Give me the diamond!" I heard Abel's voice curry through the rain. I felt a sharp weapon barely pierce my neck. Abel made his move when I was distracted. He waited for the right moment and found the perfect opportunity to strike. Damn, how could I allow this to happen? I watched my crew draw their weapons. They were just as shocked by this as me. The white guy ran towards us into view. It was Rick. "Let him go!" Rick pointed his weapon at Abel. "What do you want me to do?" Bear was talking to Smoke. I watched Smoke stand there with his gun at attention. He didn't say a word. I could tell he was deep in thought, contemplating if he should give up the diamond. My energy began to drain. I felt weaker as time passed. I couldn't speak with Abel's arm around my neck. I don't give a damn about the diamond. My only concern is making it through this alive. I'll never let him win the war. I'll kill him for what he did to my father. Rick stepped forward while speaking. "Put down your weapon. It's murder if you kill him. You don't want to do a life sentence, Abel." He looked at me. "Stay calm, I'll get you out of this kid. Abel is not the kidnapper, it's Jordan." "Don't take another step." Abel demanded. "I'll slit his throat. Hand over the diamond and we all can go home peacefully. That's my offer. Gina, get the car ready." My neck was stiff. There is no way I'll be able to rotate it to see what's going on behind me. I heard footsteps splashing through the wet grass. Abel had this all planned. He lured me here to get the diamond then escape. Is he working with The Planner? I shook the thought from my mind and focused on getting out of this situation. I was losing too much blood. "Abel," Rick said. "You don't have to do this. Put the weapon down." "Fuck it." Smoke spoke up. "Bear, give him the fucking diamond." I watched Bear turn from Smoke to me. I could feel my eyes fading from blood loss. I need to patch this wound soon as possible before I die. Bear looked at Smoke then at me. He had a concerned look on his face. He took the diamond out of the handbag. "Just give him the diamond." Rick ordered. I heard a car skid to a stop in the driveway. "C'mon," I heard Gina yell. "Let's get the fuck out of here." "Bam," Abel called. "Get the diamond." I watched Bam walk into view slowly. He approached Bear with caution. "Give him the diamond." Smoke told him. "It's ok." I saw Bear put the diamond in Bam's hand. Bam kept his eyes on Bear after retrieving the rock. "I got it." He told Abel over his shoulder. He then backed away slowly. "Big guy." I heard Abel's voice. "Help get my friend in the car."

"What?" Bear asked skeptically. "Get my friend in the car or Kane is dead." Abel's voice was harsh. "After that, I'll release him. Don't take too long. He's losing blood." Smoke spoke up. "Help put him inside the car. I'll watch your back." My eyes were blurry. I saw glimpses of Bear walking over to help Snake. He lifted Snake from the ground like he was a small child. I watched him shoulder Snake off until they vanished from my sight. I heard a car door shut, confirming Bear had done what he asked. "It's done." I heard Bear's voice. "Let him go." "Ok, Abel." Rick held his gun on Abel. "You got the diamond. Release your brother and we can all leave this situation alive." "Detective," Abel said, nonchalantly. "I plan on it." I watched Bam walk away. My eyes opened and shut uncontrollably. I felt like a newborn baby falling asleep. Abel would get away with the diamond. I had failed. I don't know how I'm supposed to face Kim or my mother. I couldn't protect them. Abel had destroyed our lives. "Abel," I barely heard Gina call out to him. "Let's get out of here." Suddenly, I felt movement. I was being dragged backwards. My air supply was less than before, I could barely breathe. We came to a stop. "Gina," Abel voice ring out. "Get the door." I felt my air supply return. Able had released his stronghold. A car door slammed two seconds later. I heard tires screeching from the driveway. I laid there on the ground under the rainfall. I didn't want to move. It seemed like the perfect place to fall asleep. I guess when you lose a lot of blood, anywhere is a perfect place to sleep. That's what they call dying, something I thought I wouldn't experience just yet. I saw four sets of boots before my eyes shut. I heard my name being called as everything went black.

Chapter 53
REBIRTH

Her vision was blurry when she first opened her eyes. She struggled to sit up straight in the bed. Where am I, she thought. Her body felt as if she's been asleep for a few days. Something didn't feel right and she had a terrible migraine. She massaged her forehead to ease the pain. She began looking around the room. Her eyesight became clearer after adjusting to the light. She realized by the surrounding, she was in a hospital. A light blue band around her wrist caught her attention. It read her name, age, and date of birth. The numbers were confusing. The admission date on the band was from a month ago. A perplexed look covered her face. She found a controller with a red button in the center. She pressed it. A nurse walked into the room a few moments later. "Kim?" A woman asked skeptically while entering the room. "This is amazing."

She walked over to the bed. "How are you feeling?" "I have a headache," Kim told the nurse. "What happened to me? This admission date is from over a month ago." She held up her wrist. "You don't remember what happened to you?" The nurse asked. "You were in a bad accident that put you in a coma. I have been taking care of you for a little over a month." Kim didn't know how to feel after receiving the information. I was in a coma, she questioned. She thought about the day of the accident. Her memory of the crash slowly came back to mind. She had stabbed a guy in the neck. That was the last thing she could remember before everything went dark. She thought about Kane. What Abel did to her was horrible. "I remember what happened that day. And thank you for taking care of me." The nurse walked over to the counter. She poured a small cup of water and grabbed some ibuprofen. "Take this, it will help with your headache." She handed her the cup and a tiny pill. "The doctor will be happy when he hears you're awake." Kim drank the water and swallowed the pill. "Thank you." She disposed of the cup. "Can you contact someone for me?" "Yes, only if they're on your visitation list." The nurse told her. "Who would you like to call?" She checked the monitor next to Kim. The display on the screen showed all signs of health was good. "Kane Simmons," Kim said. The nurse turned away from the monitor to face her. "Kane Simmons." She looked away, unable to look her in the eyes. She was aware of her relationship with Kane. He came to visit her at least five times a week. His love for her is deeper than the ocean. She saw the look on his face every time he came to visit. It was sad. "I won't be able to do that for you, I'm sorry." "What do you mean?" She was worried. "Did something happen to him?" Her first thought was Abel. He had done something to the love of her life. She couldn't live without Kane. Her heart rate increased and it caused the monitor to beep at a faster pace. "You have to calm down." The nurse told her. "Then I'll tell you what happened." Kim got herself together by inhaling and exhaling slowly, taking calculated breaths of air. The machine began to beep slower. Her heart rate returned to normal. "Please tell me what happened to him?" The nurse took a deep breath. "He was stabbed in the side of his stomach in a fight." She saw an emotional look take shape on Kim's face. "He's still alive in the room down the hall." "No." Kim didn't want to believe the nurse. "What room is he in?" "He's four rooms down on the left." She told her. "He's been in intensive care since yesterday. He was near death when they brought him in." Kim relaxed on the bed. She got the information needed from the nurse. Kane was in the room down the hall and making it to his room will be difficult. She hadn't walked in over a month. She came up with a plan to see Kane after the nurse leaves the room. "Is there something I can eat?" "Yes," The nurse said. "I'll be right back."

Kim waited for the nurse to exit. She detached the IV from her arm and got out of bed.

Chapter 54
REUNITE -KANE-

We're down four points with five seconds left on the game clock. This next play will be for the win. The crowd is going wild. We broke from the huddle. I lined up on the far side of the football field. We need to gain forty-five yards to reach the endzone. The call, hail marry. My favorite route in the playbook because I'm faster than anyone on the field. The top-ranked corner in the state lined up in front of me. He leads the nation in interceptions. He has two already in this game. The quarterback hiked the ball. I took off from the line of scrimmage. My defender was on my ass. I hit him with a sweet joke move that caused him to fall to the ground. Everything went dark. I couldn't hear or see anything around me. I held my hand up to let the quarterback know I'm open. I looked up and saw the football soaring through the air. Touchdown. I dunked the football through the goalpost. Champions. I ran to the sideline looking for my father. Everyone was celebrating, making it harder to spot him. I finally found him. He was standing there with a dissatisfied look on his face as if he wasn't happy. I stopped ten feet away from him. Something was wrong. I took my helmet off. The smile on my face was replaced with a more serious look. I approached him. He didn't say anything, not one word. He looked at me in disgust. "What's wrong?" What came out my father's mouth was shocking. "You still haven't killed Abel." I suddenly heard my name being called. "Kane." I felt my body being pushed. My eyes were blinded by a bright light above my head. I heard someone say, he's awake. I tried to move. My legs and arms felt stiff. The pain on the right side of my stomach didn't help. My eyes adjusted to the light. The room slowly came into focus. Smoke and Bear hovered over me looking like two lost puppies. "My boy is back." Bear said with a bright smile on his face. "What's going on?" I said, confused. The last thing I remember was squaring up with Abel. After that, everything else was unclear. "You lost a lot of blood." Smoke sighed. "Abel stabbed you in the side. You were rushed here in an ambulance. The doctor had to stitch the wound." His facial expression changed. "We gave Abel the diamond. It was the only way to save your life." "Bro, I'm not worried about the diamond." I told him. "You both did the right thing. I was the one who dropped my guard. I should've finished him when I had the chance."

"We'll get him." Bear spoke emotionally. "I promise." "Now isn't the time." I told the big guy. "Abel doesn't have my mother and he'll be hard to find." "What do you mean?" Smoke asked. I pressed the button to adjust the bed to an upright position. "He won't go back to the house. He's smart enough not to expose himself. He has the diamond and the notebook. My guess is he'll soon leave town. There is no telling where he will go. The first thing we should do is check the house for anything he may have left behind." "What about Rick?" Smoke asked. "He was there when we gave Abel the diamond. The police might come looking for us." "Don't worry about Rick." I assured him. "I'll tell him the diamond was fake if he starts asking questions. He thinks the Africans have the diamond, remember. I'll make up something convincing about The Planner using Abel." I don't have a solid plan to go after Abel or The Planner. Abel was prepared to put me in a box. Rick said The Planner had kidnapped my mother. I have to focus on getting her back safe. That's my next adjective. The Planner will soon make contact. His plans were ruined at the warehouse. He either wants revenge or the money, possibly both. My thoughts were interrupted by someone calling out my name from the hallway. It was a woman's voice. It sounded like Kim. Damn, am I going crazy? I wonder if I was given medicine that would cause me to hear things. Smoke and Bear held skeptical looks on their faces. They both turned to face the door, waiting for someone to appear. My heart began to race. What was I expecting to happen? Suddenly, a woman appeared in the doorway in a hospital gown. My mouth dropped. I couldn't speak. This is unbelievable. I was staring at the love of my life. A surge of energy released throughout my body. "Kim." I muttered. "Kane." She quietly said my name. A tear rolled down my cheek. She took a step forward. I could tell she was weak. Bear rushed over and gave her a hand. This is real. I've been waiting for this moment for a very long time. I don't know how to love another woman like her. My emotions began to take over as she got closer to the bed. I could see the tears in her eyes. Finally, we embraced with a passionate hug. I didn't want to ever let her go. Her heart rhythmically throbbed against mine. She couldn't hold back any longer and began to cry in my arms. "I love you with all of my heart." I don't care if my boys are around. They know how I feel about her. Their love for Kim showed on their faces. I could see the tears in their eyes. We all have love for one another and would do anything to protect our bond. I reluctantly released her, wanting to see her beautiful face. "I love you." She said emotionally. She gently caressed my cheeks with both hands and gave me a soft kiss on the lips before saying. "You know what we have to do." I knew exactly what she was saying, kill Abel.

Chapter 1
KANE TOUCHDOWN

I dunked the football through the goal post. Champions. I ran to the sideline to look for my father. Everyone was celebrating, making it harder to spot him. I finally found him. He was standing in the middle of a crowd with a dissatisfied look on his face as if he wasn't happy. I stopped ten feet away from him. Something was wrong, so I took off my helmet. A more serious look replaced the smile on my face. I approached him. He didn't say anything, not one word. He looked at me in disgust. "What's wrong?" What came out of my father's mouth shocked me. "Why is Abel still alive?" Suddenly, I heard Kim call my name. My vision became blurry for a second before focusing on the face in front of me. She was just as beautiful as the first day I met her. "You had a bad dream." She looked worried. "It was the same dream as before." "The one about your father?" She sighed. "Yeah," we were home from the hospital. It's been a month and I had this dream five times. I didn't want her to worry about me. She'd been through enough, and I won't let anything happen to her again. I would die for her. "It's ok. You don't have to worry." "Your father wants you to revenge his death. That's why you have bad dreams." She said, concerned. "You guys have been through a lot together. It shouldn't have to be this way. His soul won't rest until Abel is dead." She was right about Abel tormenting my father's soul. We had plenty of father-son moments. That day on the football field, my father congratulated me before we hugged. I remember the day vividly. I caressed the side of her face and smiled. "I know you care, but everything will be ok. I know what I have to do. Not only for my father...you as well." I broke through to her, and she smiled. "I love you, Kane Simmons." "I love you," we kissed passionately. She pulled back and slapped my forehead, playfully. "Get up, and I'll make breakfast." "Slap my forehead again if you want me to kick your butt," I joked. She popped the center of my head. "Do something." "Oh, you want me to do something?" I grabbed her waist and began tickling her. She started laughing uncontrollably and tried to escape my hold. "Ok, I got you." I pulled her closer to my body, working my fingers in every area that would make her cry. "Stop, please stop." She laughed harder and tickled my side, trying to defend herself. "No mas." "That's right," when I released my grip, she slapped my forehead and quickly sprung from the bed. "I'm gonna get you!" I shouted as she ran out of the room. I sighed. "Women." I slowly got up from the bed and stretched my arms and legs. A ray of light shined through the window, and I walked over to open the curtains in my bedroom just enough to see the morning sun. Kim and I have been staying at my house ever since Abel been on the run. My mother had been kidnapped from the hospital, so I control the property until otherwise. There wasn't a reason to worry about my brother showing up unless he wanted to die. I haven't heard anything from him. Every now and then, Smoke or Bear would stay overnight to watch for anything suspicious. We haven't made any moves with the money. Kim was shocked after I told her we have 23 million dollars. Her eyes popped out of her head when I opened the briefcase. I feel much better than before. My stab wound was healing just fine. I give it another week before I'm 90 percent. When I fully recover, I'll search for The Planner. That's the only way to find my mother in time. He wants to trade her for the diamond or the money. He might want both. After I handle that situation, I'll find Abel and put him in the ground so my father's soul can rest. I looked over to my neighbor's backyard and smiled. "My fault, big dawg." The recovery cone around the neck of the dog who attacked me looked like a lamp. I felt sorry for tossing him into a wall, but he was about to kill me. Every time I looked out of the window, he was there waiting for me to show my face to remind me of what I did to him. I shook my head. "You're not the only one who wants me dead." I shut the curtain and got in the shower. After twenty minutes, I made my way downstairs into the kitchen with Kim. The aroma in the air spoke to my stomach. Yeah, I'm hungry. I looked over at her. She was doing her thing while dancing to the music. I stepped behind and grabbed her waist. "Callaloo and shrimp? It smells good." "Thank you," she eased her head under my chin. She looked up, smiled, and kissed my lips. "I'll be back. I need to check on Bear. He fell asleep in my father's office." "He was looking for anything Abel might have left behind." She began mixing the Callaloo." "Bear," I sighed. "I told him I searched it several times and didn't find anything. He's determined to find something. Abel can't hide forever, and the police are after him. I need to find him before then." "Where do you think he's hiding?" She turned down the music. "I don't know," I said honestly. "I have a friend from high school that's helping decode everything in Abel's laptop. Asian kid, Smoke put me in contact with him." "Do you trust him?" "I don't have a choice." I picked up the spatula and tasted the food. "Delicious." "Hey." She slapped my hand. "Ok, I'll be right back." I left the kitchen and walked to the office. The door was left open, and I pushed through. I spotted Bear sleeping in my father's chair with his head down and arms crossed on the desk. "Bear, get up," I shouted as I got closer. To my surprise, it worked. Bear's head shot up from a resting position. "I'm up." He said frantically. I smirked, stunned that it didn't take any effort to wake him. Usually, I had to scream in his ear or shake him. "Kim's cooking Calloloo, it'll be ready soon ." I turned back to the door." "I had a dream." I stopped and turned around. "Me too. I had the same one about my father this morning. Trust me, we all been through hell." "It wasn't like that." He sounded serious. My facial expression changed, and I got a little concerned about the worried look in his eyes. He never before shared with us any of his dreams. The look on his face said the same. What he said next shocked me. "We were searching for Abel in Africa."

Chapter 2
JORDAN

I drove the car through the woods down a long dirt road. A log cabin came into view. The place appeared deserted on the inside. All of the lights were off, and the driveway leading up to the house was empty. I visited this place every summer when I was younger. It was where my brother and I learned to survive in the wild. My father trained us, and we became skilled hunters by the age of ten and eleven. I haven't spoken to him since I became a cop. It's been years since then. I stopped the car in front of the cabin and turned to Mrs. Simmons. It's been a month, and I thought about killing her every-single-day. She's overly beautiful, but looks are deceiving, and I'm sure she'll slit my throat the first chance she gets. I can't trust anybody, and that's how I like it. Me against the world. "This is the place." Mrs. Simmons glanced around the property. "It doesn't look like anyone is home. If you cannot hold up your end of the deal. I suggest-" "Then I'll kill you." I interrupted. She faced me, and I looked deep into her eyes when I spoke, so she felt the situation's seriousness. "Remember, you need me. I'm still debating if I should trust you. Wait here, and don't get out of the car. I don't want to put a bullet in your head just yet." I held eye contact with her for a few seconds. She didn't break a sweat at any point in our stare down. I smirked and got out of the car. Don't let your pride get you killed, Mrs. Simmons. I sighed and scanned across the front of the cabin. "Where the fuck are you?" I muttered. Not only can my brother fly a plane, but he is also a master hunter. Just not the kind that hunts animals. That's why we grew apart when I decided to pursue law enforcement. He became a hitman for hire. Flying is a part of the job. At one point in my life, I wanted to bring down bad guys like him. But that all changed when I went undercover in the Mob. Those were the best days of my life. My eyes ran up the pathway to the first step. When dealing with a man who kills for a living, you have to be mindful of booby traps. I cautiously began walking toward the front door, continuing to scan the area as I approached. "Adrian," I called out his name with my hands high to display I wasn't a threat. "Adrian, it's me. Your brother." I tried to peek through the left side window. He had smeared dirt on it. I couldn't see anything on the inside. "Fuck." He's the type of guy who knew you were at the front door. I don't know of anyone who can show up by surprise, and he wasn't aware of their presence. I heard a voice in the distance. "Try the back." I swiftly turned around and spotted Mrs. Simmons standing by the car. "Don't hurt her!" I yelled. Adrian stood behind Mrs. Simmons, ready to attack. I should have known something like this would happen if I brought her along. I'm a fucking idiot. "Ah!" She yelped as my brother grabbed her from behind and put a blade to her throat. "Adrian." I held out my hand, trying to ease any uncertainty about us being here. A surge of anxiety stormed through my blood cells. My mind said, draw your weapon and have some fun. Cat and mouse sound about right. No. Shut the fuck up, Planner! I can't get dirty right now. I have to keep Mrs. Simmons alive if I want the money. Damn, I hate saving people. Lately, I have been thinking as The Planner and agent Jordan. It's as if I'm indecisive about who I want to be. "She has a deal for you, and trust me. You need to hear what she has to say." That wasn't part of the plan, but what the hell. If he kills her, she brought it upon herself. Mrs. Simmons squirmed in my brother's arms before relaxing in his grip. There is nothing she could do to escape. My brother had control of her life. Lucky for her, she wasn't dead yet. Where was the woman I saw in the office? The crying bitch, looking for attention because someone murdered her weapon smuggling husband. She's changing by the second. I'm learning more about her fearless persona as time pass. Keep revealing to me who you really are, Mrs. Simmons. Adrian stood there without moving an inch. His eyes appeared to be black, somewhat vacant. Abel reminded me of my brother. Two lives filled with anger and death. The blade remained pressed against the neck of Mrs. Simmons, sharp enough to cut her head off. Regardless of its size, weapons used by the man in front of me are for fatal blows. Fatality is the only outcome when in war. "I'm not here to arrest you." I stepped off the porch with my hands down by my side. Fuck it. My hands needed to be by my gun. If she dies, she dies. I still have to kill Kane, if anything, for embarrassing me in front of the world. Adrian is deadly, and I had to be ready if he tried to make a move. Deep down, I wanted him to get active. "The woman you're holding can pay you more than double your fee." I stopped approaching midway to keep a safe distance, letting what I said to settle in his mind. "We need you to fly us to Africa. Her dead husband built a smuggling business. He stashed millions of dollars in a safe house, and she's the only person who knows the passcode. That's why I need her. I went out of my way to kidnap her from a mental hospital. Of course, you know I've gone rogue. I made a deal with the Africans, and they think I betrayed them. I wouldn't go there to die. She wants to hire you to fly us there, and if the situation gets dirty, well, you know the deal. This is not a one-man job. After I get my cut, you can fuck off."

Suddenly, Mrs. Simmons fell out of his grip and then turned around to face him. "He's telling the truth. I'm the only person who knows the location of the safe. My husband didn't trust anyone to help. He built the safe house with his bare hands. I stood by his side every day until the task was complete. If it's not there, the remainder of my life depends on you." My brother made eye contact with me, then put his attention back on her. "The price is triple, three million."

Chapter 3
ABEL

I walked out onto the back deck of our family beach house. Jar purchased this as a type of staycation for us five years ago. It's a shame we only came once as a family. That's what you call a father. Spend your hard-earned money where it counts. Kane is a knucklehead. He wouldn't look for me here, although I should not underestimate his intelligence. He found out I murdered our father. Brother vs. brother, I accept the challenge. My focus had to remain on getting the diamond to Africa. That's why I'm here with the rest of my crew. Kane could wait to die at a later date. There is a pilot who goes by the name Silva. His name popped up several times in the black notebook. He used to fly for Jar and made a fortune working for him. The beach house across from ours belongs to him. Who would have thought they were that close? In a matter of seconds, I found all of his information on the internet. I decided to lay low for a while until the heat died down. Only then would it be safe to fly. As of yet, I didn't come across any headlines regarding my name. I used a secure line to hack into the FBI criminal database to clear any warrants for my arrest. What is the use of being a genius if you can't use your intelligence to create an advantage? "Good morning," I heard a lovely voice from behind. I sensed Gina by my side. She leaned on the balcony next to me, close enough to touch. "Good morning to you, beautiful." I meant it. She is not like any other woman I've ever met. Her heart is just as cold as mine, and she's dangerously deceptive to anyone lower than her intellectual level. "You need to speak with Sliva today," Gina spoke in a soft tone. "He hasn't returned since last night." I didn't look at her when I spoke. The morning sun shined across the water, highlighting the breathtaking scenery. The kind of view that could win any woman's heart. "You need to rest." She said. "I'll take over and if he shows himself. I'll wake you, my love." She leaned her head against my shoulder. "Don't worry about me." A year ago, I only thought about taking over the government and becoming the underworld's unquestioned alpha boss. Gina slightly altered my perspective of women. She implements the things Jar used to teach me to be aware of when it came to women. I'm aware of the effects she has on my decision-making. I feel like I have to protect her. I wondered if this was how Kane felt about Kim when he first met her? If so,

Gina could stand in the way of a life-time awaited victory. "I won't press the issue." She said. "I think we need to get rid of Bam." The news wasn't shocking. I already knew how she felt about Bam, and I began to feel the same energy. After he left Snake for dead in the hands of an enormous freak of a man, Bam wouldn't survive in Africa. The rebels would tear him apart. I'm intelligent enough to realize she tried to provoke me to perceive that he's weak. "We can't afford to lose a brain that operates as we do. Manpower is crucial at this stage. Cutting him off now won't accelerate anything forthcoming. You need to be patient. His time will come. I promise." She sighed. "It's Silva. His boat is pulling up to the dock." My eyes followed in the direction of Gina's finger. An exotic blue and yellow four-passenger speed boat docked fifty yards away. A skinny, dark-skinned man hopped off the boat with a woman wearing a two-piece bikini. They embraced, and it ended with a kiss before they entered the beach house. The windows were open, and I could see through into the bedroom. I guess he didn't care if anyone was watching, and I've waited all night. I hope he's ready to fly.

Be On The Look Out For

My Brother's Keeper

@ Book III

ABOUT
THE AUTHOR

New York Times & International Best Selling Author
Billie Dureyea Shell was born in Compton California and now
lives in Ladera Heights with his wife and
kids who he loves to spend time with.
He is the Owner of several properties in the Los Angeles area
and gives back to his community by providing low income
housing to those who need it.
He stated "It doesn't matter where you at or where you from
it's what you do with your time. There's nothing you can't do
if you put your mind to it".